"I don't want your gratitude."

Patrick's voice was low and husky.

"But you have it," Darcy told him. "I can't stop that."

He was close now. So very close.

He stared into her eyes for so long that she was afraid she would lean toward him, show him how drawn to him she was.

Instead, he looked down to where she clasped his wrist. He covered her hand with his, turning her hand so that her palm was up. Then he brought her hand to his lips and kissed that most sensitive center of her palm.

Desire shot through her so fast she couldn't contain it.

"I want to kiss you," he said. "But if you tell me no, I won't."

She reached up and threaded her fingers through his hair. "No," she said, as she pulled him down to her and touched her lips to his.

Dear Reader

When Darcy Parrish first came into my imagination in her wheelchair, I did a double-take. Darcy could do the tango in her chair, and bake a soufflé with one hand tied behind her back. Those things are outside the bounds of my experience. I wasn't sure I could write her and do her justice. Then she opened her mouth and told me that it was okay, because she was totally unwilling to be a romance heroine, anyway.

In the meantime, Patrick Judson was hanging around at the edge of my thoughts. He thought he knew women. He'd raised three sisters. He had been running the family business for years. He was rich and powerful and there wasn't much he couldn't handle.

Somehow (don't ask how), these two managed to collide in my mind one day. I swear I never meant for them to cross paths. There was really no hope for them. But meet they did, and Darcy realised that— okay—maybe Patrick *was* handsome and intriguing, but she was still not going to go along with this heroine business.

As for Patrick, he realised that there were things he *didn't* know about women, and some things he just couldn't control. Darcy was, apparently, one of them. She perplexed him, intrigued him, and drove him nuts. But nothing was going to keep him from getting to know her better, even if a happy ending wasn't written in the stars.

Sigh. Sometimes characters just won't behave. And sometimes that's an unexpectedly good thing. In this case, Darcy and Patrick turned out to be a writer's blessing. I loved getting to know them, and I hope you enjoy their story.

Best wishes

Myrna Mackenzie

HIRED: CINDERELLA CHEF

BY
MYRNA MACKENZIE

MILLS & BOON®

Pure reading pleasure™

First published in Great Britain 2009
Harlequin Mills & Boon Limited,
Eton House, 18-24 Paradise Road, Richmond, Surrey TW9 1SR

© Myrna Topol 2009

ISBN: 978 0 263 20797 2

Myrna Mackenzie is a self-proclaimed 'student of all things that concern women and their relationships'. An award-winning author of over 30 novels, Myrna was born in a small town in Dunklin County, Missouri, grew up just outside Chicago, and now divides her time between two lake areas—both very different and both very beautiful. She loves coffee, hiking, cruising the internet for interesting websites and 'attempting' gardening, cooking and knitting. Readers (and other potential gardeners, cooks, knitters, writers, etc...) can visit Myrna online at www.myrnamackenzie.com, or write to her at PO Box 225, La Grange, IL 60525, USA.

Don't miss Myrna Mackenzie's
next Mills & Boon Romance
The Frenchman's Plain-Jane Project
Coming soon!

CHAPTER ONE

"MR. JUDSON said that his guests want to meet the cook."

"Excuse me?" Darcy Parrish's throat nearly closed up with dread as she addressed the young serving girl who had delivered the message.

"I said that Mr. Judson's dinner guests want to meet the cook."

Such simple words. Such a simple request. Why then were Darcy's hands shaking? No question.

"That's impossible," Darcy said. "Tell him no."

She looked at the young woman's astonished and horrified face. To tell the truth she was a little horrified at her audacity, too. She had only been at Judson House a week. She'd been hired by the housekeeper while Mr. Judson was out of town and had never actually met her boss. But she knew about him. She knew a lot about him.

More than that, she knew that he *didn't* know about her. At least not some important details.

"I'm sorry, I can't do that," the young woman, Olivia, said. "It would be my job. Unlike some people, *I* need this work. I don't have charity to fall back on."

Anger burned within Darcy even as she conceded that Olivia was right. It wasn't fair to hurt another person to keep from hurting herself.

"I'm sorry, Liv," she told the girl. "Really, but…I can't go out there. You don't know how it feels to be on display, to be like a bug under a microscope…I just can't."

Olivia sighed. "I'm sorry, too, but he asked, Darcy. What can I say?"

"Say that I'm covered in flour."

"But you're not."

Darcy wanted to groan. Olivia was so young and so honest. She hadn't learned the convenient little lies that helped protect a person from life's blows. And being paraded out in front of a millionaire's guests like a pet performer would be a blow, especially once they realized her situation. Pity always followed. She wasn't going through that.

"Well then, say that I'm in the midst of making dessert." That wasn't completely true, either. The dessert only needed whipped cream on the top.

"Dar-cy," Olivia drawled.

"O-liv-i-a, please. I can't. I won't," Darcy said.

"Is there a problem of some sort?" The deep, male voice echoed through the huge kitchen, and Darcy spun in her wheelchair to face Patrick Judson, her new boss, the man who had financed the group home where she was staying.

To be honest, having been assigned this job by his house-keeper, Darcy had never actually seen her boss, but who else could it be? Entering through the door nearest the dining area, he was dressed formally for dinner in stark black and white and he looked a lot like the pictures she'd seen in the news-paper. With those broad shoulders, dark, longish hair, green eyes and a granite jaw, he might have stepped right out of a magazine or a romance novel. He was definitely the kind of man that women made fools of themselves over, even beau-tiful, women with working appendages, serious pedigrees, money and no flaws. He was Heathcliff in twenty-first century clothing, and he was also…very tall.

Darcy had always been slightly shorter than average. Tall, imposing men had always made her feel squat even when she'd been able to get around well on two legs. Now, in a wheelchair, she felt even shorter, more at a disadvantage. But she'd been a fighter all her life and she'd never been one to let her fears show.

"Mr. Judson, I appreciate the offer to meet your guests, but I'm afraid that's not possible. I have to finish the dessert." Okay, that was her story and she was sticking to it.

Patrick's gaze passed around the room, and Darcy wished she could rush over and cover the obviously finished crystal glasses of chocolate mousse. But he said nothing about that. Instead he turned to Olivia. "If the coffee is ready, why don't you serve that, Olivia?"

The young woman nodded, gathered the coffee cart and rushed out, clearly glad to be spared the storm to follow.

Now Patrick turned those dark green eyes on Darcy. "How long have you been here?" he asked. "I don't remember you."

But he was studying her so intently that Darcy knew he wouldn't ever forget her. She could no longer be totally invisible the way she liked things. She fought the urge to brush away the trace of chocolate that had dripped onto her left breast. She wished she could get up and make herself tall so that she was the one towering over someone.

As if he had read her mind, Patrick pulled up the nearest stool and sat down.

Darcy's eyes widened. The man had guests, yet he looked as if he intended to settle in for a long visit!

Now, she *did* give in to the urge to fidget, clutching the armrests of her chair. "I've been here a week," she said. "My name is Darcy Parrish."

"You're from Able House."

She raised her right eyebrow. "How could you tell?" Her tone was slightly mocking and…okay, that *was* stepping over the line…in more ways than one. Of course, he knew where she was from. Everyone in this neighborhood had fought to keep the assisted-living facility for those with spinal cord injuries out of this posh neighborhood. All except Patrick Judson, who had sponsored Able House, fought for it and made sure that it was luxuriously furnished and stocked and had every technological and administrative advantage available. Darcy was grateful—more than grateful for the chance to live in a place that catered to her needs and made her feel less dependent, but she also knew that being from Able House, being an example of Patrick Judson's largess made her a marked woman and an object of pity.

For a second Patrick looked nonplussed. Then a small amused look lifted his lips. "How did I know? It's stamped on your wheelchair," he said.

Darcy looked down. "I don't see it." Of course. He had made it up.

"It's on one of the spokes."

She bent over and read the half-upside down letters on the fat, black spoke. He was right. When she looked up, her gaze met his. Those sleepy green eyes looked right into her ordinary brown ones and she felt as if she had been sucked up into a tornado of sensation. She felt helpless.

Darcy hated feeling helpless. She had been in situations where she had no control or was at the mercy of the more powerful or advantaged too many times in her life. She had been the object of Good Samaritanism gone bad before, too, and she'd certainly been forced to deal with admiration turned to pity. The times that had happened…she didn't want to remember. Not any of them. She would have none of that in her life again. Pride mattered, and she knew enough to shield herself. But now…dammit, she *liked* this job. Moreover, she needed this job.

Ever since her accident had killed her dreams of being a police officer, she had been spiraling out of control. For the second time in her life, the first being a dark period of her childhood she didn't like to think about, she had had to rely completely on the mercy and goodwill of others, and the very thought scared her to death. But here in the kitchen, with her newfound skill? She ruled. She had discovered her talent and she totally ruled. What if she lost that just because she couldn't keep her big mouth shut?

"I'm sorry about disappointing your guests," she said, trying for a humble and deferential tone.

Now, Patrick raised his brow. "Is that so?"

Okay, she had lied enough. Besides, she never lied about things that really mattered. A person's attitude mattered. "No, not really. That is, I don't want to go out there and meet them, But, I also don't want them to be disappointed in the meal."

"They're not. That's why they wanted to meet you. To tell you how much they enjoyed it."

"I…I'm sorry, but I really don't like to be on display. I just can't do that."

He nodded curtly. "That wasn't my intent."

"You didn't know I was in a wheelchair, did you?"

"I don't know you at all."

"No reason you should. I'm just another employee." Even though she knew that was a lie. When she applied for this job, Mrs. D., the housekeeper, had noted that she was from Able House, and Darcy was almost certain that the woman had favored her because of that. Not that she didn't have the talent to do the task, because she did, but this was Chicago. Talent in the kitchen abounded, and a man with Patrick Judson's money and social standing could hire the best. He wouldn't have had to give preferential treatment to a woman just because she lived at the institution where he was the chief benefactor.

But he had. Or at least his housekeeper had.

Darcy sighed. "I'm grateful for the work."

He didn't smile. Indeed, his look was grim. "If you couldn't do the work Mrs. D. wouldn't have hired you. But I have to warn you, it's a very temporary position."

Yes, she knew that. She'd been trying not to think of that. She'd been hoping that temporary meant…not temporary.

"But for now?" she asked.

Patrick leveled a look at her and she knew this was a man who was used to getting his way. "For *today*," he stressed, "I'll make your excuses. But that's a one-time reprieve. I'm leaving Judson House soon and I'll be gone long-term. When I go, every employee here will have a new place to work. That's my promise to myself, and I can't place employees elsewhere if they are insubordinate or insist on hiding their talents. If Able House is going to succeed beyond this generation, its inhabitants have to be willing to be beacons and let their lights shine, at least in some small way. They have to be examples of success stories themselves. You and I are going to work on this, Darcy."

She stifled a groan. "On what?"

"On your fear of coming out of the kitchen and meeting people."

It wasn't exactly fear of being around people that was her problem. True, she didn't like being stared at, but she wasn't a complete hermit. She just steered clear of anything that brought her undue attention, and even then…her fear was much more than that. "I don't want to be anyone's project," she said.

"Too bad. It's just become a condition of your continued employment. You're mine now."

Darcy tried to ignore the sudden quickened beating of her heart as he stood up and started to walk away.

Darcy rolled forward. "Mr. Judson. I—"

Patrick Judson turned. "Trust me on this, Darcy. I'll make sure you have security, a good job and the means to survive without being beholden to anyone before I go."

Oh, yeah, like she hadn't heard those kinds of promises before. But in the end *she* was the only person she had ever truly been able to count on.

"I don't need security." A total lie.

He paused. "What do you need?"

Darcy didn't hesitate. "I need to finish making dessert."

"Chocolate mousse? Is it good?" he asked, a teasing tone in his voice.

"Practically orgasmic," she said. Okay, that *was* over the top. The tendency to speak her mind was a good trait for a policewoman, but it could only get her in trouble here. She opened her mouth to take back her comment, but her boss had raised one dark eyebrow.

"Well, that will be entertaining, at least," he said. "I guess I owe you, Darcy, and so do my guests. That *was* a most spectacular meal. My taste buds are still humming. Thank you." He smiled.

She couldn't help it. She smiled back. How did he do that? Most likely he did that with every woman he encountered.

"My pleasure," she said. But inside, she was trembling. Patrick Judson was everything she could never have had even before her accident. The things she knew about him and the things she knew about herself…oh, yes, he was off-limits to a woman like her. So, she really couldn't do anything that implied that she was even mildly attracted. Talk about an impossible situation!

No, it was just too irritating that her new boss was so attractive and compelling. That kind of thing was just going to end right here and now.

Except the darn man was going to turn her into some sort of hobby, a cause.

Her blood ran cold. She could barely think.

"I have to concentrate on the dessert and only on the dessert," she muttered. And this time she meant every word.

She could not even allow herself to think about letting Patrick Judson turn her into a project. But how was she going to stop him?

Patrick woke up the next morning thinking about Darcy Parrish's dark, hot rebellious eyes. There had been something magnificent and defiant about her even though he could tell that she was scared and bluffing beneath the bravado. Having raised three sisters he knew the signs.

Still, he had no business dwelling on the woman despite the fact that there was something compellingly beautiful about her. He'd found himself wondering how long her wheat-colored hair would be when freed from its ponytail and…what she was wearing beneath that red apron. He could see that she was slender, but…

"Stop it," he muttered. This was completely inappropriate. She was his employee. For now, anyway, and he had sworn to help her.

Patrick nearly let out a groan. Why had he done that? His life was too busy right now and he was halfway out the door to a trip around the world. Now that his youngest sister was going off to college he was free to pursue his own interests for the first time since his parents had died and left him a guardian at age nineteen.

This trip was all he had wanted for years. He intended to grab opportunity with both hands, and nothing was going to sidetrack him, including a pair of lovely brown eyes. At twenty-nine he was still single and he had yet to sow any wild oats. He was going to do just that. Soon enough he would marry someone like himself, from his world with his goals. He would raise his own children. Angelise would be a perfect choice for a wife, and she seemed to feel the same about him. Not that they'd actually discussed marriage, yet. That would happen in time.

But for now, the family sporting goods business offered the perfect opportunity to do all the things he'd been wanting to do. The prospect of a multi-continent trip to promote the business while engaging in adventure sports for charity loomed large. No more avoiding the reckless pursuits he craved. No more being responsible for another person's well-being. He wanted that new life, badly, and it was almost in his grasp.

Except there were just a few loose ends. Able House was one, and apparently Darcy Parrish was another.

"You're an idiot, Judson," he told himself. "She doesn't even want your help."

But she would have it. He'd taken on the responsibility of Able House not only as an example to his sisters of the value of diversity in one's life, but also as an example of the duties of the wealthy to those less fortunate. The first round of residents had all been chosen as those most likely to be able to make their own ways eventually. Potential strong role models who might offer hope to others. It was clear why Darcy had been included. She was talented, bright and bold. But he'd heard her try to get Olivia to lie for her. He'd seen her anger. Something was wrong.

Having been the one to shepherd Able House into being, he had to make sure that wrong was made right. Whether he'd known it before or not, he now knew that Darcy was in his employ and that made him responsible for her.

When he left town, he had to be sure that Able House and its residents were safe from attack. He didn't want any of his neighbors to be able to say "I told you this wouldn't work" or "I told you this would be a problem" or "We don't need any trouble bringing our property values down." These were people's lives, hopes and dreams that were at stake.

He'd been lax. He'd been concentrating on getting Lane off to college and then on his own issues. Having chosen Able House's directors with care, he'd assumed that the brand-new facility had launched cleanly.

Apparently that wasn't completely true. Darcy Parrish had more than just a smart, sexy mouth. She was willing to be insubordinate to an employer rather than meet a group of people who had only wanted to praise and admire her. That could be problematic for future employers. Because while Darcy clearly had talent and could be a success, that wouldn't happen if she was unwilling to promote herself in the competitive Chicago culinary field. Patrick knew that Mrs. D. had hired Darcy because of her Able House connections. Her talent might never be fully recognized if she insisted on ignoring those who wanted to meet her. And that would be bad news for both her and Able House.

He wasn't going to let that happen. He was going to help her. And he was going to get some much needed coffee, he thought with a near groan. Damn, but he needed coffee if he was going to face the woman with a clear head.

Patrick just bet that Darcy Parrish made coffee that would make a man beg. Probably not a good idea to let her know that she had the power to make him beg, not with that saucy attitude of hers, he thought with a smile.

Oh, no. That wasn't how things were going to be.

"Let the games begin, Darcy," he whispered as he went in search of his pretty chef.

CHAPTER TWO

DARCY'S nerves were totally on edge. When she'd finally returned to Able House last night she'd been unable to sleep for hours knowing that today was likely to bring another meeting with Patrick Judson. The memory of the man's arresting presence had her mind spinning as she tried to think of some plausible reason she could give for not showing up. Unfortunately there was none. She was going to have to face the man.

"So what?" she whispered to herself. "He's just a man." And she had been working for him for a week. This should be no big deal.

Except it was. Patrick Judson was not only gorgeous and sexy, with a voice that made a woman think of…oh, things she had stopped thinking of a long time ago, he was also larger than life. And she was—eek!—going to be spending a little time with him.

No big deal, she repeated to herself again as she finally made it to work, bleary-eyed and tired. He'd probably give her a half-hour lecture and a few pointers and that would be it. Had she seriously worried that some rich guy was going to hang around with her and put her through her paces?

"Hey, Darce. So, I hear you're going to spend the whole day with Mr. Judson," Olivia said as Darcy came through the door.

So much for no big deal. "Who told you that?" she asked the young woman, but secretly Darcy was thinking, I am? The whole day?

"Mrs. D. told me that I would have to handle lunch alone."

Darcy hadn't run into Mrs. D. yet. She'd better go find out what was going on.

"But she said that it wouldn't be too difficult," Olivia continued. "Because Ms. Judson—Lane—is out shopping, and because Mr. Judson wouldn't be here, anyway. He has a meeting with you. I guess his guests were really impressed. Maybe he's even going to ask you to cater his wedding."

"Wedding?"

"Oh, yeah, I forgot that you haven't met Angelise Marsdon yet. She's pretty hot."

"I didn't know Mr. Judson was engaged," Darcy said. She thanked heaven that she hadn't let her crazy attraction to her boss show. Not that it ever would have even occurred to Olivia that Darcy might be attracted to anyone. Many people, maybe even most, assumed that the wheelchair stripped a person of desire.

"Oh, he isn't yet, but it's pretty clear that he and Angelise—don't you love that name?—are an item and that they're made for each other. Now that Lane is going to college in a few weeks, and all of his sisters will be out of the house, he'll be alone. That engagement's gonna happen. I just know it. You'll see. So, this meeting with Mr. J. is just about all that stuff last night, then?"

"Not a clue, Liv, but I'll find out soon enough. Until then, I'm really not going to worry about it." No, and she wasn't going to bother thinking about Patrick Judson's upcoming engagement, either. Still, Liv's mention of her boss's relationship with the apparently beautiful and hot Angelise Marsdon was a solid wake-up call, a smack upside the head, Darcy thought. What had she even been thinking about noticing the man's eyes and getting all gooey just because he had a deep voice and a nice smile?

"Breakfast first," Darcy said, forcing herself to stop dwelling on her boss's ability to make a woman feel hot even when she was holding the refrigerator door open. "I am not going to let you get stuck with extra chores just because I have to leave the kitchen for a few hours. Let's get started."

But she had barely managed to get the coffee made when she felt a presence at the door and turned. Patrick Judson was just entering the kitchen, and the way he was studying her...

Over the past few years Darcy had grown to expect and dread the pitying looks people sometimes sent her way, or worse, the way they glanced away self-consciously, but this was different. There was genuine interest in his gaze. And something else that made her feel like blushing when she was just not the kind of woman who blushed.

Anger sluiced through her. She liked this job. She needed it, too. Romantic or lustful thoughts were off-limits, and not just because the man was practically engaged. It went deeper than that. She'd already had a man destroy her heart when she was at her lowest. Her career had been snatched away. She'd lost her baby and more. Everything she'd dared to reach for was gone, so she no longer risked dreaming. She grasped only for the attainable. And Patrick Judson? He didn't even come close to being attainable. The man might as well have had a big, flashing Not For Darcy light on his forehead. Only a self-destructive fool would risk being attracted to him, and she was a survivor, not a fool.

Life had boiled down to the practical, the doable, and even

if she had still been the type to indulge in romantic dreams, this man was way out of her league and would have been even before the accident.

"Excuse me for invading your kitchen before you're done, but what can I say? That is one of the most incredible scents in the world," he said, glancing at the coffeepot. "A man would do a lot for a cup of that. Is it ready?" he asked with a smile that would have coaxed a snowman into a sauna.

Darcy couldn't help smiling back just a little. "It's ready. Coffee is a major food group, you know."

He grinned and that darn snowman melted a little more. "I see we share an addiction."

Darcy's body turned to fire. That deep voice and the way he breathed in the aroma of the coffee she handed him before he took a sip…Darcy could so easily imagine him nuzzling a woman's neck, breathing in her scent and telling her she smelled wonderful.

Darn it, no, where had that thought come from? Instantly she tried to blank out her thoughts. Some men could home in on a woman's attraction. She prayed that Patrick wasn't one of them. "Breakfast will be ready in mere minutes," she said, the words coming out in a rush. Thankfully the act of promising results "in mere minutes" was enough to get her back on track. The meal would have to be something uncomplicated. Omelets, she decided, with fresh vegetables and herbs and cheese.

"Sounds great," he conceded. "And after breakfast, you and I have things to do. Would you dine with me?"

Mind reading men became the least of Darcy's worries as she thought of sitting across a table from him. There was something about a meal that suddenly seemed very intimate.

"No," she said, too hastily. "I mean, thank you, but no thank you. Work to do, you know. Olivia is on her own today.

I need to…" To what? Olivia was more than capable of managing on her own when Patrick wasn't around to be fed. When Darcy had arrived, the young woman had been relying on a cache of frozen casseroles the former cook had made up. There were still plenty of those.

But this is my kitchen now, Darcy reminded herself. And she didn't like falling back on the former cook's meals. So, there. She *did* have a good excuse for not eating with her boss. She wasn't a coward.

"Work," she repeated.

"Coward," he said with a smile. "As your employer you know I'd give you a pass on the work, but…maybe work isn't the problem? You told me that you don't like being the center of attention. You must have thought I would grill you."

Darcy blinked. "Would you have?"

He smiled again. "Not until after breakfast." Then, he picked up his coffee, turned and left the kitchen. "A few minute's reprieve, Darcy," he called back. "Then you and I begin."

Silence filled the kitchen after he had gone, but Darcy's mind wasn't quiet at all. Begin what? she thought.

Less than an hour later, Patrick stood outside the house looking down at Darcy and reminded himself to tread carefully here. Darcy was his employee as well as a resident of Able House, and both of those facts made him responsible for her. It wasn't right for him to notice those warm brown eyes or the way her hair caressed her jaw when she moved. His unexpected interest in her wasn't acceptable. Especially since he would soon be leaving the country.

"Are you ready?" he asked, holding out his hand.

Those brandy eyes widened and she looked at his hand as if it was some sort of harmful weapon.

"I'm sorry. Have I…offended you?" he asked.

Quickly she shook her head. "No, not at all. And yes, I'm ready." Then she tilted her head slightly. "You just caught me off guard, that's all. People generally don't hold out their hands to me."

He nodded. "Because you need them to operate your wheels, I assume."

Darcy hesitated. "Yes, that's probably why."

But it wasn't, he could tell. What kind of people had she been dealing with? "If anyone at Able House has been unkind…"

Instantly she went on full alert. "No! They're wonderful people, all of them. I love that place! No, the handholding…I think it's just that the metal gets in the way in people's minds. It's like having one of those force fields around you from a sci-fi movie. For the record, I don't think it's an intentional snub, just an oversight."

"Good, because you would tell me if there was a problem at Able House, wouldn't you?"

She laughed. "And rat on my friends? Not a chance."

He shook his head but smiled. "You're an interesting woman, Darcy. I have the feeling there's a lot more to you than great food."

"Well, there's great coffee, too."

Patrick chuckled. "Absolutely. Now, are you really ready?"

"Not really. Last night you told me that you needed me to let my light shine. I assume that means you want me to be an ambassador for Able House. But, as I tried to explain, I'm a pretty private person. I don't think I'll ever be ready for the spotlight."

That complicated things. Could he let this drop? Not when there was so much at stake.

"I respect your desire for privacy," he said. "But Able

House hasn't had nearly enough time to prove itself to the world, and now I'm leaving. The timing isn't great, but it can't be helped. My overseas project has been in the works for five years, long before the opportunity to create Able House came about. Before I go, I have to make sure Able House's standing in the community is solid.

"That's a necessity. The people in the neighborhood have to grow comfortable with the residents of Able House, to think of them as contributors and assets. And yes, it's unfair that Able House should have a higher bar than the other locals do, but fair or not, you and your fellow residents have to show the community that the project wasn't a mistake."

The hurt, angry look in her eyes got to him. How many times had she been forced to prove herself to others?

Patrick could see the strain this conversation was having on her. Her face was pale, her body rigid.

"I'm not the only resident," she told him.

"No, but you're going to be my connection to everyone else."

"The directors?" she asked.

"Are directors. They don't have an in like you do. Caring as they are, they're outsiders. They don't live your life. They don't really know what it's like to *be* you. And neither do I. Besides, didn't you tell me that you were a police officer, a public servant? Darcy, you can still do something like that, but instead of chasing bad guys, you'll be serving Able House and this community."

While the kitchen clock ticked away, she sat there, looking angry and rebellious and sad all at once.

"You don't exactly fight fair," she said.

"My sisters would agree with you."

She tilted her head. "Were you a tough guardian?"

"A total bully."

"And not very truthful," she said with a small smile.

"Ah, the lady wants truth? All right, I let them twist me around their fingers all too often, but not when their well-being was at risk. You'll help?"

Slowly she nodded. "I don't really have a choice. Able House is special. In the short time it's been here, most of us have bonded. It's our home."

He held his hand out in a gesture of acceptance. "I promise I'll fight for you while I'm here."

This time when he held out his hand, she took it. Patrick had meant it to be a symbolic gesture, a joining, the beginning of a pact, but as she lay her slender hand in his and the pads of her fingers slid against his palm, every nerve ending in his body switched on. He was aware of her in a way he hadn't been only seconds earlier. She was no longer just a compelling, interesting woman and a great cook, no longer just his bridge to the residents of Able House. She was a flesh and blood woman who drew him in ways he didn't want to acknowledge.

He let her go as they began to move down the path toward the gardens.

"So, what do you want me to do?" she asked.

"Fill me in on your background and what life is like for you now. Give me a tour of Able House. I've been there, of course, during the building stages and at the opening ceremonies. But I've stayed away since the residents arrived. It's your home, not an institution. I haven't wanted to intrude.

"I *am* aware that some of the neighbors haven't been welcoming, and…now, after meeting you and given my upcoming departure, I'd say I dropped the ball."

"We're fine," she said.

Not true. There had already been problems with a couple

of neighbors who didn't seem to understand or to want to understand how great a barrier their parked cars posed when they placed too many vehicles on the driveway so that they stuck out over the sidewalk. Or that sprinklers that overshot the grass and hit the walkway would soak anyone rolling past. They'd been parking their cars like that for years. They'd never had to think about the impact of how they positioned their sprinklers and they resented having to change their habits for people they hadn't wanted in the neighborhood in the first place. Patrick had heard their complaints many times, and he was beginning to think that what might originally have been unconscious rudeness and laziness had become, to some extent, a form of harassment. There was still a sense that Able House would drag down property values and decrease the elite atmosphere of the neighborhood. That kind of resentment wasn't easily overcome.

"Darcy, the plan was to integrate you so deeply into the neighborhood that you become a necessary part of the whole. That would help Able House become a springboard for similar residences. But, to achieve that you have to be visible, not flying under the radar. I'm sorry if we didn't make that clear when you moved in."

"People in wheelchairs often fly under the radar."

He held up his hand. "I would never say that I understand your life, your experiences or how you feel. I don't and I can't, because I haven't lived your life, but I know this much. Your legs may not work the way they used to, but other people with functional limbs lack your talent. Hiding that talent would be a mistake."

She frowned.

So did he. "A mistake," he repeated. "Living at Able House comes with strings attached. It isn't a retreat. Retreats are fine.

They have their place, and we all need to hide away now and then, but Able House is your job as well as your home, and your job requires you to go forth and be visible. All right?"

Darcy nodded, but he could see that she wasn't happy. No wonder. She had just told him that she was a private person and here he was digging into her life.

"Has anyone ever told you that you're a stubborn man?"

Patrick chuckled. "Yes, as well as bossy and arrogant. So, are you still in?"

"I'm still here, aren't I?" she asked. "And please don't make some lame joke about how I couldn't get away. I could totally leave you in the dust if I wanted to."

"I'm sure you could," he said, and he wasn't lying. He had watched her deftly and seamlessly maneuver her chair over a place where a tree root had forced the sidewalk up a good four inches. And given her current pace, he was already taking long strides to keep up with her.

When they reached the fountain surrounded by yellow roses in the middle of the gardens, he motioned for her to stop and sat down on a bench facing her. "All right, here comes the part where I'm not only stubborn but pushy and nosy as well. So, how did you end up at Able House?" he asked.

"Don't you already have all that information?"

"I don't intrude on the residents' lives."

She gave him a wide-eyed look of disbelief. Given all that he'd told her and the demands he was making on her, he could understand her incredulity.

"Okay, I didn't *intend* to intrude. I carelessly assumed everything was going as well as could be expected, given the neighbors' initial reluctance. I didn't realize that there might be any other complications until you told me that you didn't want to be visible. And, okay, that stuff about not butting in?

I'm making an exception in your case," he agreed. "But I'm not digging through your files or asking one of the directors to break trust with you—which they wouldn't do, by the way. I'm just…asking you. I won't know if you leave something out."

Darcy frowned. "So, I could lie to you…"

"And I'd be clueless."

"That wouldn't be very helpful, though, would it?"

He laughed. "No, it wouldn't."

"So, you're trusting me?"

"Looks that way." He waited.

She gave him an incredulous look. "That is so lame. How did you ever grow up to be such a success? In the part of town where I grew up, you would have been taken advantage of on a daily basis."

He gave a casual shrug and continued to wait.

"I hate that you're trusting me. It means I have to be honest. I do have a code of honor."

Now, he couldn't contain his grin.

"You knew that, didn't you?" she asked.

Patrick tipped his head. "The directors spent a lot of time choosing the residents. Honor would have been important and they would have gone over every detail of your situation, your personality and your accomplishments. They probably know things about you that you don't even recognize yourself."

Her frown grew. "I doubt that very much, but…all right. I'll give you the abbreviated version of how I came to be where I am. I wasn't always in the chair, only for the past couple of years. Actually I was born in a very poor part of the city and ended up in an experimental suburban school program where a group of us with meager means but a decent stash of brains were thrown in with the cream of the elite. We were *not* welcomed or popular, as you might imagine, but the leaders of the program patted themselves on the back for helping the disadvantaged, the elite parents patted themselves on the back for allowing us to mingle with their children, the teachers patted themselves on the back for having to put up with our presence—the administrators hated the extra paperwork. Knowing that we were unwelcome charity cases, we had chips on our shoulders and bad attitudes, and the other students barely tolerated us. In addition, the district had budget cuts and the following year we were sent back to our own neighborhood schools where we were considered to be uppity for having mixed with the rich kids. The whole experience left me with a bad attitude about certain types of philanthropy."

"And you think Able House is like that?"

"No, but I don't like to be held up as an example or a poster child."

"Understood."

She gave him a small, resigned smile. "But we're still going forward with this."

This time he couldn't smile back. "Darcy, I was nineteen when my parents died and I was left to raise my three sisters. If I've committed myself to a cause or to individuals, I don't want to be like those people who dropped your project after a year. I intend to follow through and make sure that Able House will survive whether I'm here or not."

"Well, then, you've got your woman. Survival is something I know all about." Her smile and her attitude practically blew him away. He had a feeling it would be dangerous to underestimate Darcy Parrish. Or his reaction to her.

CHAPTER THREE

WELL…this was certainly stressful, Darcy thought as she and Patrick continued on, proceeding down the path toward Able House. She was constantly aware of the man by her side. In a physical way. In an emotional way. She hated losing control of her emotions, but her unexpected and completely feminine and foolish reaction to Patrick Judson was leading her to do just that, and now he wanted her to—

"All right, here's the rest of my story," she said, rushing ahead in the hopes that reliving those bad old days would smack some common sense into her. "After that wonderfully humiliating experience I told you about, I turned into a rebel, got in trouble, but quickly realized that was a road to disaster. Eventually I somehow got my act together enough to get into and graduate from the police academy, but just as I was about to achieve that dream, I ended up in a one-car accident that left me with some sensation but minus the ability to walk and chase down the bad guys. And then…a few things happened and I ended up here. So there, now you know everything about me."

His smile was warm, even as he shook his head. "I said that I was going to trust you. I didn't say I was a fool. *Some things happened, and you ended up here?* All right, I won't ask for the details, but it's obvious even from that brief introduction that you're a much more complex woman than you care to admit. So no, I don't know you."

"And *I* don't know you."

"Touché. I'm asking you to share, but not reciprocating?"

"I'm not complaining. You're not really my business, are you?" she challenged.

"Maybe not, but I'm asking a lot of you. So, what do you want to know about me?"

"Why did you fight to get Able House into the neighborhood? Why does it even matter to you?"

Patrick stopped walking. "Partly selfish reasons. My life has been taken up with my sporting goods business and my sisters, and when Lane—who is eighteen and heading off to college—was in a serious accident and we didn't know what condition she would be in six months down the road, I had to wonder what her life would be like if I weren't a rich man or if I weren't around. How would the world treat her? What opportunities would she have? Who would she become? Would the world even realize what a gift she was? And, when I mentioned my concerns to a physician friend and heard that there had been interest in starting something like Able House for several years, it was an easy choice to donate the land and the money. But, I would never have thought of getting involved at all if my sister hadn't had the misfortune to have a skiing accident." He shrugged.

But Darcy wasn't about to let that pass. "Lots of good things wouldn't happen without a catalyst or a defining, life-changing moment. I haven't run into her, but I assume she recovered."

"Completely."

"I'm glad." Without thinking she reached out and touched his hand. Instantly awareness of him as a man kicked back in full force. Warmth, pulsing energy, a frisson of excitement ran through her. Was she insane? She'd barely been able to sit still when he'd been holding her hand earlier. Now, *she* had initiated contact? The instinct to jerk away was strong, but she couldn't let him know that one totally innocent brush of her fingertips against his skin had affected her this much.

"Almost to Able House," she managed to say. As if he didn't know that.

"Lead on. You're the expert here." His low voice resonated through her body. Darcy kept moving, hoping none of her friends would notice how flustered she was.

"Hey, Darce, why are you back so soon?" someone called out as she rolled within view of the center. "Aren't you working?"

"Detour of duties today. We have a visitor," she said, happy that her voice sounded reasonably normal. As they neared the building, which was surrounded by deep green lawns, winding walkways, fountains, flowers and sculpture, more people appeared. All were in wheelchairs.

"Is that Mr. Judson?" one older man whispered to the man next to him, loud enough to be heard.

The other man smiled. "Sure is," he said. "You've seen his pictures in the paper and he's been here before."

"But he's with Darcy," the man said.

"Edward, you know I work for Mr. Judson," Darcy said, raising her voice a bit because Edward's hearing was less than perfect.

Still, everyone looked a bit perplexed and concerned. "I know what you're thinking. I didn't mouth off and get fired. He isn't here to return me for a better product."

Patrick chuckled and everyone turned to look at him.

"She's an excellent product," he said to Edward. "Not the

type to be returned as unacceptable. A great cook. Have you eaten her chocolate mousse?"

"Oh, chocolate," Maria said, her voice worshipful. "I love that stuff. But ask her to make you a lemon meringue pie next. It's better than sex."

Instantly Darcy felt uncomfortable—and hot. She was afraid to look at Patrick but she did it, anyway.

"Better than sex? Well, I wouldn't want to miss that." he said with that lazy tone that made Darcy feel shivery. For some reason the fact that she even felt that way when he talked made her angry.

"People think that a person stops thinking about sex when they have a spinal cord injury, but we don't," she said defiantly.

"Why should you?" Patrick asked. "Sex is complicated. It involves the mind, not just one or two body parts."

Darcy noticed that Maria was looking at Patrick with lust in her eyes. In fact, she was looking very much like a woman on the verge of propositioning the man, and Maria was a beautiful redhead, an intelligent and capable woman.

"Now that we're all settled in, Mr. Judson is here to learn the ins and outs of Able House. He wants to make sure we're well established when he goes overseas soon, and he might be expecting us to go out in public and do some promotion," Darcy said, a bit too primly.

"Hey, okay by me. Whatever Mr. Judson wants," Maria agreed.

Patrick looked a bit uncomfortable. "For starters, I hope you'll all call me Patrick," he said as Darcy made the introductions and Patrick shook hands all around. Later, when they were alone and back at the house, Darcy repeated the details he wanted.

"Edward is an electrical engineer. Maria is a computer

programmer. Cerise was an Olympic swimmer who now teaches and coaches at a local fitness center. Laura is a fashion designer. Aaron is a dentist. If this weren't the weekend, most of them wouldn't be here. They have jobs." Her tone was a bit defensive, she realized.

"I'm not the enemy, Darcy," Patrick said, sliding to the floor beside her wheelchair.

"I know you're not the enemy," she said. "But I—I feel as if you want something from me that I'm not sure I can give and I don't even know what you want from me yet. Do you?"

"Not exactly. I want to know that you're fine."

"I am. It's been rough those first two years, but I've learned so much."

"Like what?"

She got a sly look on her face. "Well…I can pop a wheelie." She did so with ease. "And I can move from my chair to a standard chair in record time." She pointed to a chair normally used by one of the staff and transferred herself back and forth quickly from one chair to the other and back again. "If I have to, I can get this puppy up a step if it's not too high," she said, patting the bicycle tires she favored on her chair. "In short, I can be a real person, Mr. Judson, and get along without help. I'm fine."

But his green eyes were stubborn. "I want better than fine. Don't get me wrong. I'm awed by the fact that you can manage in ways most people couldn't, but those reluctant, inconsiderate neighbors of ours…"

"They want celebrity," she said. "Ceremony. Pretty wrapping paper with all the trimmings. If I were a rock star who just happened to be in a wheelchair, they'd welcome me."

He didn't look away from her direct gaze. "You're right and I'm not about to apologize for them. They're wrong."

"But you still want me to…to what?"

"I want you to make them envy you, to show them that the community would be diminished by the loss of all of you."

"We shouldn't have to do that."

"You're damn right about that," he said, angrily. "But if I get overseas where I'm not in easy reach and someone hires some legal eagle team and tries to do some workaround scheme to close down Able House…I'm trying to prevent them from even wanting to attempt that. That's all. All right?" he asked.

Darcy pursed her lips and gave a reluctant nod. "If you put it that way…if we're gearing up for a fight of sorts…" Her words ended on a harsh laugh and she looked up and blinked, trying not to show her frustration. Sometimes it felt as if she'd been fighting all her life. For money. For respect. For the right just to exist.

"I'm not trying to punish you, Darcy," Patrick said, and he cupped her jaw with his palm, kneeling next to her chair. "Really. It's not like that at all."

His hand against her skin produced an instant reaction, an awareness of him as a man. Darcy struggled to think to continue breathing. "I know you're not trying to punish me," she managed to say. "I'm so…grateful for Able House. All of us are. Couldn't you hear it in their voices when they spoke to you today?"

"I don't want you to be grateful, although I appreciate the thought. I want you to…not have to justify having your home here."

"But we will, won't we? Just by having to take the extra steps other people don't have to take, we'll work for the right to stay."

"Yes, and it's not right," he said with a groan, sliding to the ground beside her.

"What are you doing?" She looked down at him.

He looked up at her and smiled. Her heart thumped. "Making myself short," he said. "Do you mind?"

She laughed. "Well, I've gotten used to looking up people's noses, but no, I welcome the chance to look someone other than my friends at Able House in the eye."

"I'll remember that."

No, don't, she wanted to say. *Don't be too nice to me. Don't make me want things I can't possibly have.* Because she had once had things she wanted and had them taken away. Love had been one of those things.

She tried not to think of the other thing, the unborn baby she had lost and that terrible day afterward when she had lost that last sliver of faith that she could ever try to become a mother again. Darcy fought not to remember all of that…and failed.

"So, why are you going overseas?" she asked, wanting to change from the subject of loss to something more positive.

Patrick shrugged those big, broad shoulders. "It's time. I've been running the company for years, raising the girls. Now, they're grown and I have things I've put off that I want to do. I'm twenty-nine, still single, I run a major international company that sells sporting goods, but while I love adventure sports and risk-taking, I haven't taken any risks."

Darcy gave him an "are you kidding me" look. "I thought you said you raised three sisters. Sounds like risk-taking to me."

To her consternation, he moved closer, resting his arms on the side of her chair so that he was very close. "Are you teasing me, Darcy?"

No, she was torturing *herself.* But she wasn't going to back down. "I'm just saying it couldn't have been easy."

He moved away and went back to leaning against the wall. "I loved it, totally, but…you have no idea."

"No. I've never had any children." And never would now. Not after losing her baby in the accident, not when she wasn't going to get married, ever, and not if she couldn't be the kind of mother she wanted to be. So much for avoiding that heart-constricting pain.

She looked up and saw that Patrick was studying her closely. So, she dove into survival mode and forced a smile. "So, tell me more about your upcoming trip."

He continued to study her for a few more seconds.

"Please," she said.

He nodded. "It's one of those trips that's the result of too many years of daydreams. Probably too long and too expensive and too monumental in scope, but I can't wait. Several months spread out over a number of continents. Part of it will be spent on business and part will be a series of charitable fund-raisers built around adventure sports. We're hoping to draw big crowds and really make a difference."

He held out his hands. "It's a very meaty venture, a long time in the making, and yeah, I'm pumped, even though I feel just a little guilty. It sounds as if I couldn't wait for the girls to grow up so I could have a life."

Darcy leaned forward, closer to him. "Why should you feel guilty? You've worked hard, everyone knows your company is a success. You raised your sisters and…how old are they?"

"Twenty-five, twenty-three and eighteen. Cara and Amy are married and have children of their own."

"Well, then, there's no problem, is there? They're grown, and they're not going to care what you do."

Patrick gave her a look of disbelief. "You haven't met my sisters."

No, she hadn't. But that changed a few hours later when the doorbell rang, and she heard the sound of footsteps in the hallway. Lots of footsteps. She'd been told to prepare food for a few extra mouths, but it sounded as if an entire army had arrived.

She and Olivia exchanged a look. "It's them," Olivia offered.

As if she knew who "them" was. "Who?" Darcy asked. "You've been here longer than me. I don't know the code yet."

Olivia rolled her eyes. "The sisters," she whispered as the voices grew closer.

Darcy barely had time to panic before the kitchen was filled with tall, dark-haired, gorgeous women and…a dog? A big dog?

"Fuzz, get down," one young woman ordered as the dog pounced, setting his paws on Darcy's lap. Startled, Darcy dropped the stainless steel bowl she was holding. It rolled around on the floor, clanging.

Immediately a cacophony of high-pitched feminine voices began. One of the beauties screeched.

"Oh, no," another one said.

"Patrick is going to have a cow," the third one said.

"Fuzz. Down now." Patrick's voice broke through the noise. The sad-looking, big-eyed mutt backed off of Darcy.

"Later," she told the dog, winking. "Steak."

"No steak," Patrick said.

"Tyrant. He's just a big puppy."

"Who doesn't belong in the kitchen," he insisted.

We'll see, Darcy thought with some amusement. She'd spent a lifetime being told she didn't belong here or there. She and this dog had something in common. But Patrick had turned his attention away from the dog who had wandered out of the room.

"Cara, Amy, Lane, what were you thinking?" he asked, crossing his arms.

"We thought you were in here," one of them said. "We didn't think about Fuzz. Come here, big brother. We have a secret to tell you." She looked down at her abdomen and smiled.

"Cara? Another baby?" Patrick's voice was soft. He folded his sister into his arms.

"And she's such a baby when she's having a baby," another sister said. "Mark my words, she'll be calling you whenever there's a crisis."

"I will not!" the other sister said.

"You did when you were pregnant with Charlie."

"That's because I was looking for an excuse to come over and give Patrick a hand with you, Lane, sweetie," Cara said. "*You* are a handful."

"At least I won't come running to Patrick when I have a husband the way you two do," the youngest beauty said.

Immediately the two older sisters began to protest and the ensuing sounds was nearly earsplitting, but Patrick calmly broke in. "Enough. You haven't said hello to either Darcy or Olivia yet. Or apologized for letting Darcy be attacked by Fuzz."

Darcy started to open her mouth to tell him that Fuzz hadn't hurt her, but Patrick shook his head.

The trio of beauties greeted Olivia and turned to Darcy. "We were out of line," Cara said.

"We weren't thinking," Amy agreed.

"And we really are sorry," Lane agreed. "You're new, aren't you?"

"As new as they get," Darcy agreed with a smile when Lane held out her hand.

"What happened to Elaine, the last cook?" Amy asked.

Patrick gave her a look that clearly indicated that was an off-limits topic.

"Ah, the usual," Cara said.

Darcy raised one brow, but she said nothing other than what she felt needed saying. "I hope you'll enjoy what I've prepared for dinner."

"I'm sure it will be great," Amy said.

"Yes. Absolutely," the other women said.

"All right, we've disrupted Darcy's kitchen long enough," Patrick said. "If she's going to work her magic, she needs us out of here."

"Magic?" Lane asked.

"Darcy is a veritable genius in the kitchen," he clarified, winking at Darcy.

The sisters exchanged a look. Not a happy look, either. "Is Angelise coming?" Cara asked. It was clear that she wanted the answer to be yes.

"I didn't invite her," he said.

"Why not?"

Patrick frowned. He didn't answer. Now Darcy was as curious as his sisters were, but it wasn't any of her business, was it? Besides, if he wasn't going to share with his sisters, he certainly wasn't going to tell his cook his secrets.

But as the sisters and Patrick left the kitchen, Darcy was certain she heard one of the young women say, "Be careful about how you praise Darcy, Patrick. You know how many members of your staff have fallen in love with you? One word of praise and they're writing Mrs. Patrick Judson in their diaries. It's not fair to hurt them or lead them on."

"I have no intention of leading Darcy on." Had Patrick really said that or was that simply what Darcy thought she heard? His voice had been muffled and low.

"Olivia?" Darcy asked. "Is that how I got this job? The last cook went off the deep end over…um…Mr. Judson?" No matter what Patrick had told everyone at Able House, this was not a good moment to start calling him by his first name.

"Afraid so. They *all* fall in love with him. I would, too, but he's too old for me."

"Well, you don't have to worry about me. I'm not falling

in love with anyone, least of all my boss. I don't go looking for trouble anymore."

"Yes, but my mother says that sometimes trouble just finds us."

"Not me."

Olivia shrugged. "Whatever you say, but I've seen it happen over and over. That last cook—Elaine? I liked her, but she was practically stalking Mr. Judson. He had to let her go."

A sick feeling ran through Darcy. She knew all too well what rejection felt like. "We'd better get the meal on the table. We have four mouths to feed."

"Six."

"Who else is coming?" Darcy asked.

"The baby-sitter is on her way over to drop off Mr. Judson's nephews, Charlie and Davey. They're just four and five and so cute you just want to pick them up and hug them. They're the light of Mr. Judson's eyes. He loves children."

"Children?" Panic attacked Darcy's senses. She fought against it.

"Yes. Like I said, two of them. You'll see."

Darcy shook her head. "No, I'll be in the kitchen. You'll be serving."

Olivia gave her the look. "You know Mr. Judson might want you to put in an appearance."

Darcy wanted to say no, but she couldn't do that. She had had her one reprieve. He wouldn't allow her another. Like it or not, panicked or not, she was going to have to enter a room filled with women who were wondering whether she had a crush on Patrick, she was going to have to face those babies she couldn't bear to face and she was going to have to do it all while trying to pretend that Patrick had absolutely no effect on her at all.

CHAPTER FOUR

TWO HOURS LATER, Darcy blew out a long breath. She had made it through the evening. Barely. Every time she'd entered the room, she had had to decide where to look. Those two gorgeous little boys were at one end of the table. Just one glance had nearly made her heart break and made her wonder…would her child have had those chubby little elbows, those huge, innocent eyes? The pain she thought she'd conquered had hit her like a sledgehammer, dredging up emotions she'd learned to suppress.

Darcy only hoped her hastily pasted-on smile had hidden her distress. Her inability to face children was not something she wanted to discuss.

After that, she had avoided looking toward the boys and had concentrated instead on doing her job and on the adults. Whenever she'd entered the room, Patrick's sisters had seemed to be talking about women. Specifically, Patrick and women. More specifically, Patrick and Angelise Marsdon. Apparently the lovely Angelise was quite a catch. And no question about it, Patrick was…he was…

An image of smoldering green eyes and dark hair assailed her. Sudden, unexpected heat suffused Darcy's body, and as if her physical reaction was like some sort of magic beacon, she heard Patrick's telltale masculine steps nearing the kitchen. Caught off guard, she felt the plate she'd been holding slide from her hands, and she had to practically throw herself from her chair to catch it before it hit the floor.

"Darn it!" she said, hugging the expensive piece of china to her chest.

"Are you all right?" Patrick's deep voice was laced with concern as he came through the doorway. Darcy braced herself for the physical reaction she felt whenever he was near. Not a surprise. Probably every woman on earth had that same reaction. It was meaningless, she reminded herself as she nodded at him.

"I'm fine. I just nearly broke a plate that probably cost more than a Mercedes."

He frowned.

"It's all right, though," she said, holding out the plate to show him.

"I don't care about the plate," he told her. "That's not what's worrying me." But obviously something was.

Patrick was angry. At his sisters but also at himself. It had been obvious all through dinner that Cara and Amy and Lane had an agenda where Darcy was concerned. Angelise's name had been mentioned several time in Darcy's presence, and while the food had been melt-in-your-mouth perfect, his sisters had offered only the most rudimentary of compliments and they had maintained a distant air.

"I'm sorry," he told Darcy when everyone had gone home. "They're grown up and yet despite two of them being married and mothers, they're still young in too many ways. I'm sure I made some mistakes and indulged them too much to make up for their lack of real parents, but their manners are usually much better than this. I'll talk to them."

Darcy shrugged. "What did you expect them to do? Faint over my apple tart?"

"A few oohs and ahs wouldn't have been misplaced. It was the stuff men have killed for, and that cinnamon scent wafting off of it…" He groaned.

Darcy's eyes opened wide as if she was startled, as if he had done something sexual. Well, maybe he had. There was something very sensual about a woman who smelled like cinnamon and vanilla and could create masterpieces with those talented hands of hers.

Abruptly Patrick shut down those thoughts. What in hell was he doing? Darcy was his employee. As such, there were barriers he wouldn't cross.

"Your sisters were perfectly polite. They said the food was very good."

They had, but these were the three sisters who had been born speaking in superlatives. Something was amiss. He had the feeling he knew what it was. Darcy was prettier and more talented than any of his other cooks had been.

"My sisters have decided they're going to choose a wife for me, and you're an attractive woman. I think they see you as a potential wrench in their plans."

And that blush did amazing things to her skin. Dammit, he had to stop thinking like that. Where were his principles and his self-control?

"They were disappointed that Ms. Marsdon wasn't invited," she said.

"I know. Angelise tops their list. They've been trying to match me up with her for years."

"Are you going to allow yourself to be matched?"

He raised a brow.

"Sorry," she said, looking sheepish. "Cop training. Be direct, get to the point. Wade in and ask the tough questions."

"Do you miss it?" he asked, then shook his head. "No, don't answer that. None of my business."

She laughed. "I just asked you if you were going to get engaged to a woman I've never met. You're my boss and I'm asking you personal questions. And you're apologizing to me for being nosy?"

"All right. I'll be nosy. Do you?"

She looked him straight in the eye. "I wanted it very badly. I was good at it. It meant getting respect. I was going to do something important. I was going to save the world. But that's all done now."

"Don't make the mistake of thinking that what you do now isn't important."

"I cook."

"You feed people, you nourish them."

"Oh, you're good. No wonder your sisters are worried that every woman you hire is going to fall in love with you."

He gave her a look, tried to think of what to say, tried *not* to want her to be a little bit interested in him so that he could get closer to her so he could taste that sassy mouth.

No.

Had he thought that or had she *said* it?

"No, don't worry. I'm not going to fall in love with you," she said. "When I had my accident I was engaged to be married."

She hesitated.

"I see," Patrick said. Or at least he was beginning to. Who was that guy, he wondered? What kind of an obtuse idiot had he been?

"This isn't something I talk about," she said, her voice dropping to a mere whisper.

"You shouldn't have to. Your privacy is sacrosanct, Darcy. I promise you that. I won't ask."

She looked up and stared directly into his eyes. "If this is going to cause your sisters even one moment of concern, that can't be good for anyone. I don't want there to be strife between you and your sisters or concern about my role here, so they—*you*—need to know that I'm not some starry-eyed romantic looking for love. After my accident, my fiancé…well, suffice it to say that I'm not stupid enough to start down that road again." Her body was rigid. Her pretty brown eyes were troubled, and it was obvious how uncomfortable she was discussing this, but she had done it to reassure him.

Patrick had to work hard to control his anger. "It sounds as if your fiancé was the stupid one. Some men don't deserve what they're given."

She sat stone-still for several seconds. Then she sucked in a long, visible breath. "So, are you going to marry Angelise Marsdon?" she asked, catching Patrick off guard. Clearly she wanted to change the subject. Only a total jerk wouldn't take the hint.

"I don't know. Maybe. Eventually. Now that the girls are grown I'll eventually marry someone and Angelise and I have been friends for a long time. We grew up in the same world. We have similar interests."

"Does she like risk-taking and adventure sports, too?"

"She likes to ski."

"Well, then…"

"You sound like my sisters. Your next words should be 'why not?' And my answer is not yet. I have things to do."

"That trip. *Your* dream."

"Yes, although…I feel a bit guilty putting it that way. That makes it sound as if I begrudge my sisters the time I gave them. I don't. I love them. I love my nephews, too, but…I apologize if they made you uncomfortable. I know they stared at you when they came in, and I can see their presence unnerved you."

She shook her head vigorously. "Don't. They're perfectly adorable little boys. Beautiful children. And of course they stared. They're children faced with a new person and a new situation," she said, indicating her chair.

"But you could barely look at them, and it's not acceptable for them to make people uncomfortable with their curiosity. Young as they are, they need to learn that."

"I—do *not* do that."

"What?"

"Make your nephews feel guilty about staring at my chair, or apologize or anything like that. It's not them. It's me. I'll admit that…I'm just not very comfortable being around children."

He nodded. Lots of people weren't comfortable with children, but it was clear from the look in her eyes that her reaction was something out of the norm. It was also clear that Darcy didn't want to discuss the details, and he had no right to push.

"All right. I won't make them feel guilty. I never intended to do that, anyway. They're far too young. But Charlie and Davey and I might still have a bit of a man-to-man talk. Guy stuff."

She sighed, then smiled wearily. "They'll probably wrap you around their tiny little fingers."

"That's a good possibility," he admitted.

"And you'll love every minute."

"That, too."

Finally she smiled, and Patrick felt as if the sun had emerged after a long, gray day. "Come on, I'll walk you home," he said.

He could have sent for the Able House van. It would have been the wise thing to do, given his current mood, but he didn't want the evening to end on this somber note.

Still, in the dusk, as the sun began to set and the stars began to glow, the darkness closed around them and he was aware of the woman beside him in ways he didn't want to be. Her scent drew him.

"I shouldn't have told you any of that stuff about myself," she said quietly. "I don't usually open up that way but I guess it was only right that I spill some of my own secrets since I was being so nosy myself. So…here's a question. I made an appearance outside the kitchen tonight. Are we done yet?"

Her voice was low and husky and warm, she was only inches away from him as they walked along.

Suddenly he stopped.

She did, too, and without even thinking, he dropped down beside her. Her toughness, her fragility drew him, scalded him. He knew she was amazing, complicated in ways he hadn't even begun to discover. She had layers he couldn't even imagine yet, but she was breakable, too. That toughness was a cover. Now that he knew that, he…

Patrick looked down at her and the pale starlight lit up her brown eyes, that beautiful face. She was so very alive and warm…and waiting for his answer.

"We're not done yet," he said. "And without allowing himself to stop and consider the inadvisability of his actions, he leaned in and touched his lips to hers.

Her silken hair brushed his fingertips as he cupped her jaw. Her lips were enticingly warm, achingly moist and she tasted of cinnamon and something uniquely her. Patrick wanted to come back for more. Instead he pulled abruptly away.

"I'm sorry. That was a mistake," he said. "I don't harass my employees."

She shook her head. "I don't feel very harassed," she whispered.

"What do you feel?"

"You don't want to know, because you were right. It was a mistake. You and I—no—not even for fun. You've got your trip, your business, the freedom you've been waiting for, all those adventures you're going to have and those kids that Olivia says you want someday. My plans are completely different. I'm definitely not going for the husband and children. And crowds? No, thank you. No spotlight of any kind for me after we finish saving Able House."

He leaned back and crossed his arms. "Still, you should have a full life. More than just cooking for some rich guy who lives alone."

"Hey, I like cooking!" she protested.

"Shh," he whispered, smiling down at her. "It wasn't the cooking I was objecting to, just the audience you have. You may not like crowds, but you should at least get more exposure than you get working for me.

"Attracting some additional exposure would be a good starting place. Able House needs to build a reputation, and you've got an extraordinary talent. We need to find an alternate workplace for you, anyway, so…let me do a little homework. Then we'll take on the world."

It was a good idea, he thought as he headed for home. He'd rather take on the world than risk wondering why he kept wanting to kiss her again.

And he did want that very badly. Her skin had been so soft, her lips so warm…

Patrick groaned.

"Wrong time, wrong place, buddy," he told himself. He and Darcy were headed in opposite directions.

In a few weeks he would leave and might never see her again. But he would remember the taste of her and her take-no-prisoners spirit for a long time.

When Darcy arrived home two days later, she realized immediately that something was different. There was a buzz in Able House that she hadn't felt before. Not that the atmosphere here wasn't positive. It was the most homey place she had ever lived. Even when she'd been able to walk around on two legs she hadn't experienced the energy that existed in this place. But this morning something was happening. She knew it. Her gut instincts, the ability to feel a change in the stratosphere, in the mood of her surroundings that she'd honed on the street and at the police academy took hold. And pretty soon the reason for that change, that extra energy became apparent.

Cerise came rolling up to Darcy. "Hey, Darce, we're expanding our horizons."

"What do you mean?"

"Classes, training, public speaking."

"I still don't understand," Darcy said.

"I don't, either, but it has something to do with your Mr. Judson."

"Not mine," Darcy said automatically, but even as she said the words she remembered how his lips had felt against hers the other night. She'd felt…claimed. She'd felt…dominated, but in a good way. She'd always hated being dominated. It made her claustrophobic and rebellious, but when Patrick had touched her she'd just sat there, enjoying the tingle and the closeness and the warmth and the man. His hand had lightly cupped her jaw and she hadn't even objected.

Which was downright scary. She remembered what Olivia had said about the cooks that had come before her, and she didn't want to follow in their footsteps. Letting herself wish for things or reach too high was a recipe for disaster. Especially given the fact that Patrick was her benefactor.

Every time she had wanted something badly or been a recipient of someone's good ideas, she had always lost. That ill-fated school experience had severely damaged her pride and made her a target. Her abandonment by her fiancé, an instructor at the academy who had encouraged her to apply and claimed he would love her forever had made her question her ability to judge people. And her baby...oh, her baby who had never known life...

Darcy closed her eyes. With that tragedy she'd lost her sense that life was mostly good even if some of it was bad. If she even thought about Patrick as anything other than her boss...disaster was a certainty. If she knowingly did something so stupid, she risked her self-respect and her last chance to find happiness and purpose.

"Darce, are you okay?" Cerise was waving her hand in front of Darcy's face.

"Perfect," Darcy lied. "What do you mean by classes?"

"Not the usual kind," Cerise said, rolling her eyes sarcastically. "Patrick—you *know* it was him—called up Mr. Baxter here in the office and grilled him on some enrichment possibilities. He's set up some tutoring opportunities with the best in their field. Dancers, elite chefs, experts in new technological advances, wheelchair racers, swimmers, designers...you name it. If one of us wants to take a class—and Mr. Baxter said that he really hopes that as a gesture of faith in what Patrick is trying to do, we'll all devote ourselves to studying one new thing—an expert will be found to teach us, at no

charge to us. But, that's not all. The two of them are also ar-
ranging some charitable ventures."

"I don't understand. This is already a charitable venture,
and you just said…"

"This second part isn't charity for *us*. It's charity given *by*
us. We're supposed to take our gifts and our expertise out in
the world and use it by volunteering to teach, to aid, to make
a difference. Twice a month if our schedules allow for it.
Patrick will arrange for the initial contacts and once he's
gone, Mr. Baxter will be our liaison. I'm not sure I understand
all this, but it's very cool."

"He's trying to make us examples," Darcy said.

Cerise frowned. Darcy didn't blame her. Being held up as
a poster child to enlist sympathy and oohs and ahs was a two-
edged sword.

"I didn't mean that the way it sounded," she quickly told
her friend. "He wants us to show the people in this area that
losing us would leave a hole in their community. He wants us
to be contributors, accomplished public figures."

By now a few other people had gathered round. "That's
never going to happen," one person said. "Patrick practically
had to cram Able House down people's throats. Now that we're
here, the demonstrations may have stopped but very few people
are really welcoming us. They don't criticize. They'd feel too
guilty doing that, but they don't want us here in their elite
neighborhood, either. We're an island cut off from the rest of
the community by a wall of silence. Patrick can't change that."

Darcy wanted to object, but she didn't. Because she was
sure the man was right, and this lingering conflict wasn't fair
to Patrick. He had sacrificed all of his adult life and had
earned the chance to be unencumbered. When he went off on
his trip he shouldn't have to be worrying about Able House.

Darcy didn't know how to change that situation, but she knew how to change her part.

"Let's take a look at those classes. If Rick Bayliss of Frontera Grill is teaching a class," she joked, "I am so signing up right now."

To her surprise, he was and she did, but…that wasn't really pushing her boundaries, was it? She had to do more, to show Patrick that she could be bold and fearless and fine once he had gone. Closing her eyes, she gathered her courage. Then she took her pen and signed on the line next to the class that frightened her the most.

Wheelchair ballroom dancing. She'd been a heck of a bad dancer back when she had legs that operated smoothly.

"Sounds like fun," she told the person next to her. Although it didn't. It sounded scary. Darcy hated being in situations where she might look foolish, where others might stare at her, but…this was all about pushing limits. She had always been about pushing limits.

Besides, if she wanted to administer a knockout punch to the fear that she was becoming too attracted to her boss, she had to replace it with an even bigger fear.

"There's a recital at the end of the class," she muttered. Panic attacked her, and for one whole hour she didn't think about Patrick at all.

But then she did. And why not? She was on the way to his house where she was to spend more time with him. He'd left a message on her voice mail and asked if she would be available. He had news about the plans they'd discussed the other day.

Available? I'm feeling way too available. Darcy hated even admitting that, but it was true. "Please let Patrick leave town soon," she prayed.

CHAPTER FIVE

PATRICK looked up from his desk to see Darcy in the doorway of his office. "I got your message, so here I am. Is this about…the other day you said we were going to take on the world," Darcy said.

Her chin was high, her lovely hair falling back to reveal a long, slender neck that drew his attention, reminding him that in some ways he was no different from any other red-blooded male. There was a look of bravado plastered on her pretty face, but Patrick could tell that it was a show. Her hands on the wheels of her chair were white-knuckled.

His heart went out to her. "I might have been hasty in demanding that much," he said, wanting to give her an out. They could start more slowly.

She shook her head. "What day does your trip begin?"

He named a date just a few weeks away.

"The world it is, then," she said. "No point in mucking about and wasting time."

He smiled and shook his head. "All right, then. You win."

She grinned. "Sweet. I like winning."

Patrick couldn't help laughing, then. "I'll bet you were a handful growing up."

She shrugged, avoiding the comment. "Um, Mr. Judson?"

"Patrick," he said. "In spite of our employer-employee status, I think we've moved beyond formalities."

For a minute she look flustered. He probably shouldn't have reminded her that he had kissed her or that she had revealed heart-deep secrets to him, but he hated having her call him Mr. Judson.

"All right, then. Patrick," she agreed. "What exactly are we planning to do? What does taking on the world mean?"

"Dinner party. Big. Some names you'll recognize from the news and the society pages. I want you to prepare the 'meal of your heart.' Then I want you to put on your best clothes and cruise the room, let people chat you up."

She went rigid, her lips practically turned blue, she fanned herself with her hand. "I have to tell you that I stink at the chatting me up bit."

"Darcy," he drawled. "You'll do fine. Just be yourself."

"You have got to be kidding. I was going to be a street cop, dealing with hardened criminals. Decorum is not my strong suit."

"But chocolate mousse is. Rich people love their food, and above all, they like discovering the next new thing. They'll love you."

She rolled closer. "I'll bet you were a good big brother. Did you always encourage your sisters this way?"

He sat down in a chair right next to her, staring straight into her eyes. "I was flying by the seat of my pants every step of the way with my sisters and I didn't have a clue what I was doing. Even though I tried to be a good parent and to be encouraging, I don't even want to think of all the mistakes I made. Somehow they survived."

"Oh…but they love you. I heard the way they talked about you."

He laughed at that. "They certainly had their moments when they hated me, too. Trying to discipline a fifteen-year-old when you're only nineteen doesn't exactly make you popular."

"I can imagine it doesn't. But you did it, and you stayed."

"Of course, I did. I'd do it again. I wouldn't even leave now if I thought they needed me to stay, but they don't. They're all grown up." Patrick couldn't keep the pride from his voice.

"You're such a dad," she teased. "So…adventure sports? What does that entail?"

"Rock climbing, paragliding, white water rafting, snow-boarding, that kind of thing."

"You can do all that?"

For a second he thought he heard a wistful tone in her voice. "I attempt all that," he said.

"Sounds dangerous."

He grinned. "You sound like the girls. They don't exactly approve of me risking my neck, but since the entry fees and other monies raised from the events go to promote extracurricular sporting programs for kids in disadvantaged areas, they understand."

"So, in a way you're just substituting being a dad for your sisters to being a dad for a whole lot of other kids."

"Ouch! Don't nominate me for sainthood yet. Yes, this is a great cause, but I also love pushing my limits and I haven't allowed myself to do much of that for a long time."

"Now you can," she said softly.

"Yes." But he realized that *she* couldn't do most of those things. Not anymore. But the things she *could* do were amazing, like fighting back from a serious injury, creating meals that were out of this world delicious, feeding people, sassing a man when he needed sassing…

Aw, don't go there, Judson, he warned himself. *Next step you'll be staring at those lips again.*

"Let me tell you the basic elements of the party," he said, trying to take his mind off those lips. "I'll leave the details up to you."

"Are you sure you want me to put in an appearance?"

"I want other people to experience the Darcy Parrish taste."

He'd meant food, but now he *was* looking at her mouth.

She nodded, but then she froze. "You *do* have a reason for this dinner party other than me, don't you?"

Okay, he could lie, couldn't he?

Patrick wanted to groan. How could he lie when she was looking at him like that? "Sorry. This is strictly a coming out party for your talents. A job audition," he said, leaning in and crowding close to her. "And don't get that mutinous look in your eyes, Darcy. When I'm gone, you need a new position. I want you to have a good one."

"Patrick Judson," she said, poking him with her index finger. "I may not be ambulatory and I may have to occasionally rely on the kindness of others, but I do not want to be a charity case. I don't want to do this like some pitiful contestant in a cooking contest in the hopes that someone might like me well enough to choose me."

He caught her hand, enclosed it in his palm and brought it to rest on his heart, cupping her gently, keeping her still. "Not you, Darcy. Them. *They're* the contestants. You're the judge."

She shook her head, looking up at him with wide, worried eyes that glistened with her anger and frustration.

"I'm sorry," he said. "I'm so sorry. I thought you understood. You're not the one on display. They are. Any one of them would be lucky to get you. All you have to do is talk to them, see who you might feel comfortable working with and make your choice."

She closed her eyes. Was she going to cry? What a jerk he was. What an idiot! "Darcy," he coaxed gently. He brought her hand to his lips and kissed her fingertips.

Her eyes flew open wide, and he saw that she wasn't crying at all. "You," was all she said. "Oh, Patrick," she went on, laughing. "You—only you would think that I would be the one making the choice. Don't these rich people have cooks already?"

He knew he should let her go. Instead he leaned closer. "Oh, that isn't going to matter. You are the best. Believe me."

She sat there gazing at him and then she leaned forward and kissed him on the cheek. She raked her palm across his cheek, so that he wanted to turn his head and kiss that palm, make love to that soft skin. "I do believe that you're slightly crazy, Patrick," she whispered. "I should call your sisters and tell them how crazy you're talking, so they can get you some help, but I won't. I—it seems I have a dinner party to prepare."

"Darn right you do." He released her and she moved away, headed toward the door. "My guests are going to fight for the privilege of hiring you." The end result would be a new employer for her, he hoped, but at the same time there was a hollow feeling of loss deep in his chest.

"It's nothing," he whispered to himself after she had gone. He was just imagining things. Because he really wanted this trip he'd been planning for so long. He wanted freedom and a life he'd chosen, not the one that had been thrust on him. And then when that was done, he would settle down with a wife, someone who understood his world and welcomed it. They'd have a house full of children and a nice normal life. That would be perfection. Wouldn't it?

* * *

Had she actually kissed Patrick on the cheek when they had already agreed that any kind of touching would be a mistake? That was far too risky. The man was her boss! Enough of this being attracted to him already, Darcy told herself the next week as she planned the party, attended her first ballroom dancing lesson, discovered that she loved it and attended another.

She wondered if there would be dancing at the party. Patrick had said that she was planning it, but he had been talking about food-related details, not the rest. She wondered who would be there. Patrick had given her numbers. He'd handpicked most of the guests but allowed his sisters to invite some of their friends and acquaintances as well. Undoubtedly she would know no one other than the Judson family, but given Patrick's social standing, there would probably be people she'd heard of.

Darcy tried not to think about being introduced to people who would consider her either inferior or worse, an object, the token disabled person. She'd been that too many times, but…she shook off the bad feeling.

And yet…what should she wear? Oh, no, how could that little detail have skipped her mind? She hadn't concerned herself with her clothing in years. Expedience and comfort had been paramount, but now…

"Olivia, help!" she said. "What should I wear to this dinner? Do you know anything about style?"

Olivia turned to Darcy with a sly smile. "Darcy, does ice cream make my butt look big, and do I eat it anyway?"

Darcy blinked.

"The answer is yes," Olivia said, grabbing her arm. "And right after work we're going to go through your closet, your jewelry box and your makeup kit and then we're going shopping. You are going to knock Mr. Judson and everyone at that party on their wealthy...um, behinds."

Uh-oh, she'd released a fashion monster, Darcy thought. Her question had been innocent enough. She hadn't expected so much enthusiasm. "I was thinking of something a little less major than knocking people on their behinds," she volunteered.

Olivia gave her one of those "don't argue with me" looks. And Darcy had to admit that even in the kitchen Olivia strutted her style.

"Okay, you win," Darcy said. She hoped she wasn't making a mistake.

Two days later on the eve of the dinner party, she was sure she had made a mistake. The kitchen was under control, the extra staff members were following her directions. The tables, the silver, the candles, the china, the linen...everything looked perfect. But Darcy, having just emerged from an Olivia-style makeover, glanced into the mirror in front of her and wondered what she had been thinking.

The dress was perfect, a pretty slate-blue with a portrait neckline. A single wide gold chain framed her neck, and her hair had been styled into a chin-length breezy, swingy style. Unaccustomed to makeup, she had blush on her cheeks, lipstick on her lips, eyebrows that had been plucked and shaped, eyelids that had been tastefully shadowed. She felt elegant in the dress, but glancing in the mirror and then down at herself, she had one thought.

"They'll notice the chair first," she said.

"So what?"

Darcy had no answer for that. Olivia couldn't possibly understand.

"Yes, so what?" a deep male voice asked. A voice that went right through her and made her ache.

Darcy turned to face him. "You're making me meet them. I'll meet them. I even understand why and I'm grateful, but…the chair…"

"It's a great looking chair."

She frowned.

"Darcy," he said slowly, and he gave a brief nod, a signal that sent Olivia out of the room with a smile. "Maybe Olivia and I can't ever really understand completely. Neither of us can be in your shoes or know what you're feeling or what it must be like to be you, but for people who didn't know you before your accident, the chair is a part of you. And since it helps you do all the things you need to do, it's a good part."

"I know that. But—"

"What?"

"I don't want people to give me a pass because of the chair, to be easier on me because of it. The meal has to stand on its own. I don't want anyone waxing effusive because they think I need to hear pretty compliments."

He thought about that for a minute. "I can understand that. So…"

"So, I don't want anyone to know anything about me until after the meal. And if the results aren't positive—such as someone saying that my bouillabaisse sucks, then I stay in the kitchen."

"Darcy," Patrick drawled.

"Patrick, please."

"I get to make the call," he said. "I know them better than you and I can read their reactions."

She hesitated.

He waited.

Okay, fair was fair. Patrick was, after all, doing this for her. "Agreed," she finally said, feeling the butterflies starting to form.

"And Darcy," he said, as he turned to leave. "Your bouillabaisse is fantastic."

"I know," she said with a grin. "Too bad I'm not making that tonight."

"You'll pay for that," he warned with a sexy smile.

She waggled her fingers and shooed him out of the room…and waited.

He was magnificent. Darcy had heard snippets of the conversation from her station in the kitchen where she had thrown on an apron and was personally making sure that the meal was perfect. Some of the names Darcy had heard were household names, yet their deferential tones told her that they looked up to Patrick.

For his part he was gracious to everyone. And he had kept his promise. Once the meal had begun and everyone had been escorted to the dining room, Darcy had been left to do her job in anonymity. Of course, that meant that she didn't have a clue as to what was going on in the other room. The servers seemed to be good at their jobs, but they were keyed in on their work. It wouldn't be right to try to get them to spy or to pump them for information.

The strangest thing was that while Darcy knew that the exalted of Chicago society were eating her food, she was more nervous about how Patrick reacted to the meal than any of them did. And she'd been cooking for the man for several weeks now! That alone told her that she had stepped over a line she didn't want to cross.

But how to stop caring what he thought?

"Just stop," she muttered.

A server passing by looked up startled.

"Oh, no," Darcy said. "You're doing fine. You're doing great. Go on."

"Darcy."

She glanced up, fear gripping her as she heard Patrick's voice. The moment of reckoning was here, and there wasn't any way to put some positive spin on this. Either the response had been tepid and she would have to live with the knowledge that Patrick was disappointed or it would be positive and she would have to roll into the other room and meet that sea of faces.

"It's time," he said and he held out his hand.

She moved forward, stopped and took his hand.

"You're sensational," he told her.

"Patrick, I can't—not like this. It's too—I'm too—people will stare at me." Suddenly every humiliation of that long-ago day when she had walked into that exclusive prep school came rushing back at her. Her gym shoes had been on their last legs, because her mother hadn't been able to afford new ones yet. Her clothes had been the best she owned but still thrift shop specials. As she had moved past that sea of squeaky clean kids with their designer clothes and their expressions that told her that curious as they were, they would not be inviting her to any parties, she had wanted to run, to get out from under the microscope. She'd wanted to beg them not to look at her, but…

Those old, bad memories broke into pieces as Patrick dropped to his knees in front of her. "Darcy," he said. "I would never knowingly humiliate you. And…"

He frowned, that chiseled jaw growing harder. "Dammit, I don't have any real right to play God with your life or to presume to know what you're about or what you've been through, but I know this much. You have an amazing talent and a skill that no one else in that room possesses. I watched them, Darcy, while the meal was going on. They were in gastronomical heaven."

Darcy gave him a skeptical look. "That's pushing it, don't you think, Patrick?"

He shook his head slowly, his eyes never looking away from hers. She wanted to reach out, to frame her palms around his face, to feel his skin as he spoke.

"Not far enough," he said. "I know it's true, because I was so intent on catching their expressions and their comments that I almost missed the meal myself."

"Were you worried that I would mess up?"

He grinned and reached out and took her hands in his own. "Not even remotely. The scent of your cooking, Darcy…"

He groaned, a sound that made Darcy hot, then cold, then hot again. She snatched her hands away for fear she would do something stupid. The man certainly had a heightened olfactory sense, didn't he? And wasn't there just something incredibly…sexy about that?

Don't think that. Don't ever think that, she ordered herself. She tried to turn her attention back to the mundane.

"Your cooking was one of the hot topics during dinner," Patrick continued. "You may not recognize all the names, but everyone in the room has a reputation for discriminating taste in food. Yet I have it on good authority that Donovan Mintner rated your vichyssoise six stars on a five-star scale and Eleanor Givelli went off her diet for a half hour so that she could have a second helping of your lemon plum cake. Michael Brisbin asked me where I'd found my chef and wondered if there were any more where you'd come from. The point I'm trying to make, Darcy, is that they're already half in love with you."

"With my cooking."

He got that stubborn frown that she was beginning to recognize. "I have a feeling that your cooking comes from your soul. It's definitely more than a skill you've learned, which means that yes, it's *you* who has captured their hearts."

"Stomachs," she said just as stubbornly.

Without warning, he reached out and stroked his palm down her cheek, smoothing back her hair. "Didn't anyone ever pay you any compliments?" he asked. "You seem so unwilling to accept them, even when they're the truth."

Darcy fought against closing her eyes to drink in the sensation of his caress. The answer to his question was yes, she had earned compliments over the years. Just not like this. Not from someone who had opened a window to her soul. Not Patrick.

Save yourself, a little voice inside her whispered. *Run away.* And because she'd spent a lifetime relying on her instincts and had been part of too many situations where her feelings had been out in the open and ruthlessly trampled, she did just that. Darcy rolled backward just a touch. Just enough.

Patrick lowered his hand. "I'm sorry. I didn't even ask before I touched, did I?"

"I suppose it was kind of a big brother thing. You know, once you're in the habit of nurturing, you can't turn it off." Darcy desperately needed to believe that, because thinking of his touch any other way, even beginning to daydream was…preposterous, potentially heartbreaking. Unthinkable.

His brows drew together. "No, it wasn't like that," he said, as if half to himself. "Not remotely like that." He rose and took a step backward. "But you're right. It probably should have been. Dammit, we don't have time for me to get remorseful and apologetic right now. I can hear rumbling in the other room. They're probably wondering where I am and if I've bundled you off somewhere so they won't get a chance to steal you. I told them I would bring you."

"Oh, no. Are you saying that there's a sea of people waiting to meet me? I thought we were just going to quietly slip in and you might introduce me to a few people and then I would leave. This sounds like a big production."

"Nothing wrong with doing things big."

Of course, she should have expected that. This was a man who ran an international company, who had taken on the gargantuan task of raising three girls when he had not been much more than a child himself. This was a man who was organizing a global charity venture which entailed him jumping out of airplanes, rocketing down mountains on a tiny board and who knew what all else?

"Big? If I weren't so grateful for your help, I would roll over you with my chair." The words just popped out before she could think to stop them. Immediately she pressed both palms to her mouth. "I didn't just say that, did I?"

But Patrick had tipped his head back and let out a hearty laugh. "Oh, yes, and I'm not forgetting it, either." He laughed again, and Darcy heard sounds coming from just beyond the door.

"They must wonder what we're doing in here."

"I'll bet they'd never guess that you're threatening me with bodily harm," he teased. "Come on, we'd better go. And Darcy?"

"Yes?" She barely got the word out. She was a mess, a complete mess.

"It's probably best to watch your temper. I want them to hire you, not run away for fear you're going to trample them." His smile was broad and teasing and…just too darn sexy. That wasn't fair, not fair at all when he was as unattainable as the moon and stars.

"Don't you even see the chair?" she said in frustration.

His teasing grin faded. "Of course," he said. "I also see your eyes. You have the most amazing, expressive eyes. I'm pretty sure I saw a few sparks fly from them a few seconds ago."

Warmth puddled in her heart. Nonsensical desires and questions racketed through her brain. She had to ignore them, but...no one had ever spoken to her like this before. No one had ever made her feel like this. "What else do you see?" she asked, knowing it was the wrong thing to ask.

"Oh, so much more," he said, his gaze skimming down her. She felt heat everywhere he looked. Her face, her throat, her breasts. "But it wouldn't be a good idea to mention those things when other people might hear."

For a second she thought she saw frustration in his eyes, but then he turned and moved toward the other room. "Your fans await, Darcy," he said.

CHAPTER SIX

WAS he making a mistake doing this, Patrick wondered as Darcy entered the room. He knew how much she disliked being the center of attention. He also knew that she would be weighing every stare, analyzing every comment. What on earth had the world done to her? And that guy she'd been engaged to, what kind of a man would walk away from a woman like this just because her legs would no longer support her?

Idiot, he thought. But he didn't have time to pursue that train of thought and, anyway, it wouldn't be wise to even go there. Darcy's beauty haunted him, her frankness enchanted him, the fact that she didn't seem to be even remotely impressed or in awe of his money and social standing made him wild to get to know her better. And her body…well, as he'd told her it was better not to think those kinds of thoughts. It was best not to think of her in any way other than as a talented woman he was committed to promoting. Because he was leaving.

He had to leave. He'd waited all his life to leave. He'd put off everything for the girls' sake. And now that the trip was near, he had made commitments, big-time commitments. His company, his reputation and the future of a whole host of charities that were relying on his help were tied up in this venture.

It was his pleasure to go, but also his duty, and he had learned about duty at an early age.

Besides, he had no business bringing Darcy too closely into his world. It was one thing to handpick a group of guests, tactful, good-hearted people with deep pockets, who would treasure her and be careful with her. It was another to subject her to the public scrutiny she would face if anyone ever thought that she was anything more than just his chef.

The public and the media were often unkind. They peeled back the outer layers to expose the vulnerable stuff beneath, and…he had no idea what all Darcy had gone through in her life, but he knew that she was vulnerable beneath that tough exterior. A person didn't develop a tough exterior unless that person had been forced to protect herself. No doubt anyone who had to go through the harrowing experience of losing the use of their limbs and muscles and all that that entailed, who had had the rigors of excruciating physical therapy forced on them, developed strength, but Darcy had holes in her armor. If it was up to him, he wasn't going to let anyone near enough to expose those holes.

And he certainly wouldn't allow himself to do anything that might harm her…including letting the world know that he was attracted to her.

But he couldn't ignore her, either. That would be worse. And it would be suspect, as well. He had brought this group here tonight to meet his prize chef, whether they knew it or not. Then, he had taken it a step further and promised them an introduction. Darcy's future lay in the balance.

Showtime, Judson, he told himself. He gave Darcy a smile and moved forward to meet his guests who were gathered in small groups in his parlor having after dinner drinks.

He made a beeline for Eleanor Givelli. She was his first

choice, a warmhearted woman with a large checkbook. "Eleanor," he said, as Darcy moved forward. "Allow me to introduce Darcy Parrish, the woman who created that lemon plum cake you admired."

Eleanor was a short, plump woman with springy red curls. "Darcy? How wonderful to meet you. And I didn't just *admire* the cake," she said, laughing and gesturing with her hands, sending those red curls bouncing. "I attacked it and devoured it. No shame at all. It was delicious, as I'm sure you know. Not that I'm surprised. Patrick only has the best in his life. From employees to friends to…oh, everything. The girls, you know. He always had to have the best for them, to only expose them to people who met his high standards. He certainly knows how to zero in on talent."

"I—thank you. I'm so glad you enjoyed it," Darcy said, looking pleased but a bit overwhelmed by the woman's effusive charm.

Patrick began to move on.

"Oh, you're not taking her away, are you?" Eleanor asked. "I wanted to speak to you, Darcy, about an affair I need catered in two weeks. And don't get all possessive on me, Patrick. I know she's yours, but you're only one man, and Lane is a tiny woman and probably not even here all that much, given her social calendar."

Patrick grinned. "Are you telling me that you're trying to steal my chef?"

"Not yet," Eleanor said. "For now I just want to borrow her to cater this affair I'm having. And maybe one or two more."

"Are you sharing, Patrick?" Michael Brisbin seemed to appear from out of nowhere. "Because if you are, I'm first in line behind Eleanor here. My company is starting to plan its summer bash and your genius of a chef here—" he gave Darcy a smile and a nod "—is miles above the one we've used in the past. I'm Michael, by the way," he said directly to Darcy. "And you are…"

"Darcy," she said with a smile. Michael was a genius and a good man but he had the tendency to speak a mile a minute.

"Beautiful," Michael said, and Patrick gave the man a sharp look. The word hadn't sounded like a simple response to having finagled a talented chef's name. He had sounded like a man meeting an intriguing and beautiful woman.

"Hey, Patrick, don't scowl at me like that. Didn't you hear Eleanor? If Darcy isn't averse to sharing with us…do you have an exclusive right to her?"

No, he had no right to her whatsoever. Furthermore, he had arranged this dinner in the hopes of bringing about just this kind of response.

"Darcy is a free agent," he said.

"Free agent. Did someone say free agent? Are they talking about you, Patrick, darling?" Angelise asked, coming up and linking her arm through his. "Because if that's true, I'm staking a claim on you. I haven't seen you in weeks. Fortunately your sisters knew how I was pining away and invited me here."

Patrick blinked. Not in surprise, exactly. He'd known that his sisters had invited Angelise and he had spoken to her at dinner. They'd known each other for years, were good friends and he'd even occasionally—as late as a week ago—thought that after her divorce was final and she was free, the two of them might consider becoming closer. He *did* want to get married eventually, to have children, and he and Angelise had a lot in common. Similar backgrounds, similar interests. They would suit.

But tonight wasn't about him and his plans. It was about

Darcy, and his sisters had known that. They had championed his support of Able House. He'd assumed they might have dropped at least a hint of this night's purpose to Angelise. She would have known that he had duties and wouldn't have time or the inclination to flirt right now. What's more, after having known him forever, she was aware that he preferred to do his flirting in private.

"Angelise," he said, "I'd like you to meet Darcy."

Darcy smiled and held out her hand. "I'm afraid I'm the free agent, but maybe Patrick is as well."

Now it was Angelise's turn to blink. "Patrick, is it?" she said. "I didn't know that he was on such familiar terms with his subordinates."

Patrick opened his mouth to protest, he saw Darcy's quick blush and his sisters' startled, panicked looks. Angelise had never been haughty.

"Darcy is an artist. She's not my subordinate," he said.

But Darcy gave him a sad, resigned look. Then he saw her—did no one else see her?—paste a completely phony look on her face. She laughed and looked at Angelise.

"You're right. I'm afraid I'm a bit of a rebel," she said, her voice laced with humor even though Patrick could read tension in her eyes. "I don't always play by the rules. Staying in the kitchen keeps me out of trouble most of the time, though. As a matter of fact, I have to go there now. I just came out because…Mr. Judson requested it, and he is, as you say, my boss." She gave Angelise a nod as if to say "you've won."

But as she turned to go, Patrick stepped forward. "You just got here," he reminded her.

"Yes, dear," Eleanor said.

"We'd enjoy talking to you, picking your brain, getting to know you better," Alex Torres, a young, handsome man added.

He was looking at Darcy as if she was on the menu and Patrick wondered what had possessed him to invite the man.

A chorus of those in agreement with Alex chimed in.

Darcy's smile was grateful but there was a stubborn set to her chin. "Thank you so much, but I have things to finish."

Patrick felt the first threads of anger weaving their way through him. He had cajoled Darcy into this situation, and now she had been made to feel uncomfortable. He would talk to Angelise, of course. He would apologize to Darcy, but the damage was already done. And she wanted to make her escape. He really should let her go, but—

"What do you have to do?" he asked, persisting.

"I have treats to package up," she said in a stage whisper. "Cream puffs and éclairs."

"Oh, my hips and thighs," Eleanor moaned. "Darcy, you're killing me. Let her go, Patrick. By all means, but I want your business card, Darcy. In fact, I want multiples. When Patrick leaves and you have more free time you're going to get so much business."

"Yes, me, too," someone said, and the words were echoed.

"Tomorrow," Patrick promised. "I'll make sure you get her cards."

Darcy thanked everyone and began to leave the room. Just as she was halfway through the door, he moved up beside her, touching her shoulder.

She stopped.

"We're not done," he told her. "This isn't finished. We'll talk later."

Darcy was in the kitchen, all the guests but Angelise and his sisters had gone home, and Patrick had to face the fact that there was unpleasant business to attend to. It was a fact of his life and had been for more years than he could remember. A man-boy didn't successfully raise three sisters without having had to force himself to deal with challenging or unpleasant situations from time to time.

"You three, wait for me in the study," he told his sisters. "And Cara and Amy, don't try to tell me you have to get home to your husbands and babies. I know that Lewis and Richard have a late-night game of poker, and Charlie and Davey are safe in the care of Mrs. Teniston who will care for them as if they're her own, so you've got time to give me five minutes."

"We're not children anymore," Amy pointed out, but they all came in and sat down. "And I do want to get back to Davey. I miss him when I'm gone."

Patrick sighed. He knew she meant that and he sympathized. He'd felt the same when he'd had to leave the girls with a sitter. "All right, I'll make this short," he told them. "I don't know what was going on tonight with Angelise, but I know you were at the heart of it, and I don't want it to happen again. Darcy was embarrassed, Angelise was acting out of character and you appeared to be interfering."

Lane put her chin up. "You should know that we never meant to hurt Darcy and we'll tell her so, but…we had good reasons."

"Really? I'd like to hear what they were."

"We told you. We saw you looking at Darcy the other night and especially tonight. You're attracted to her."

He didn't even try to deny it.

"Has it occurred to you that you might be leading her on? Have you thought about how disastrous it would be if she fell for you?"

"That isn't going to happen."

"Women always fall for you. You don't choose any of them. Or at least you haven't while we've been growing up.

We know it's because you didn't want to really date and lead us through a series of potential moms that might not pan out. But surprise! We're grown now. And you can choose whomever you want, but we know it won't be Darcy."

Anger began to simmer, but he controlled it. "How do you know that, Cara?"

"I'm not criticizing Darcy, but…we just know you, Patrick. You've been waiting all your life to take risks and now you can take them. Besides, I know you love us, but the weight of being responsible for us has to have gotten to you at times. No matter how independent Darcy is…you're her benefactor. You've aided her. Won't that be more of what you've been doing for us for years, the very thing you're breaking free of? Plus, if this went wrong, we—it would be different from an ordinary breakup simply because you *have* been her boss and benefactor. If you felt that you'd hurt her in any way while she was under your care…we know you, Patrick. It would kill you. You'd eventually do something unwise in a bid to make it right for her and end up sacrificing yourself."

He opened his mouth to protest, but Lane rushed in.

"Look, we know you've said you're not even going to think of marriage until after your trip is over, but you're totally free to date as much as you please. And eventually one of the women you date might become your bride. You've always said that when you marry it will be to a woman who shares your background, your interests and your ambitions, and that means someone like Angelise who's from your world and who likes climbing mountains and reckless pursuits as much as you do. And you want children. You've always wanted children, but Darcy—when we were here the other day she couldn't even bear to look at Charlie and Davey. I don't think she wants babies."

Patrick ran an impatient hand over his jaw. He didn't know why Darcy seemed to fear contact with his nephews but he wasn't about to discuss her private concerns with his sisters.

"We're sorry, Patrick, but…we just want for you what you want for us—a carefree life and someone to share that life."

"All right," he said, raising one hand. "You've made your point. Now, stop. All this worrying about Darcy…it's meaningless. She absolutely doesn't want to get married to anyone. She isn't interested in a relationship."

The three of them exchanged a look, the kind that said their sister antennae was turned on.

"I'm sorry, but we just don't believe that. At least not where you're concerned. You have this way of making women forget what they don't want and simply home in on what they do…which is you."

Patrick thought about that. Did Darcy want him? Maybe a little, in a physical sense, but…his world, the press, the attention…how long would it be before some callous idiot of a reporter wrote a story about how she was after his money or about what a great guy he was for hooking up with a disabled woman? One moment like that—and there would be many moments like that—and Darcy would retreat back into anonymity somewhere, scarred for having consorted with him. He would have harmed her just by showing her attention.

"You don't have anything to worry about," he told his sisters. "Darcy and I aren't going to get involved. I can promise you that."

Darcy was packing up to go when Olivia sidled in wearing a crestfallen look.

"Olivia, what is it?"

Olivia hesitated. "I don't know if I should tell you what I overheard, but…I don't know if I should keep it from you, either."

But Darcy did. Whatever it was that was bothering Olivia was a burden to her. "Spill it," she said.

Olivia began, haltingly, to relate what had been said in the room adjoining the one where she had been cleaning up, including the comment about children, a topic that made Darcy want to shout that she wanted babies. She just couldn't bear the thought of not being the kind of mom she had dreamed of. She couldn't live with the thought that if her child climbed the stairs, she couldn't rush up them to prevent him from falling down the steps. "I'm sorry, Darcy," Olivia said. "I just…his sisters are great people and so is Mr. Judson, but you should know that the girls are matchmaking, that they think you're falling for him, but they don't think you're right for him."

Darcy felt sick, but she couldn't have Olivia feeling guilty for telling her something or start worrying later that what she had revealed to Darcy had hurt her. And, if there was one thing that Darcy had learned it was how to put on an act, to pretend that she was fine with the blows life sent her way, to keep her chin up so that her pride could survive. She was good at it, too. No one could tell that she was lying.

"Oh, Olivia," she said, smiling and holding out her arms. "Come here, sweetie. I can't believe you're worried about something as silly as that."

Olivia came close. Darcy took Olivia's hand and smiled up at her friend. "Believe me, Olivia, while I like Patrick, we tease each other and he helps me, he's just my boss. A great boss, but no more than that. As a matter of fact, tonight I collected a bunch of phone numbers for people who want me to cater their parties, so, if anything, Patrick and I will be spending less time together, not more. Gosh, Liv, he's handsome as all get out and yes, like most women I can fantasize about what his lips taste like, but heck, I feel that way about any number of movie stars, too. Don't you?" Somehow she managed a convincing laugh, and Olivia hesitated, then smiled and joined in.

"Thank goodness, Darcy," she said. "So…you really have no interest in Mr. Judson?"

"Patrick might be on my 'ten hottest men' list, but he's not on my list of men I plan to date, no."

"So who is?"

Darcy managed not to gasp. Olivia spit out the water she had been drinking. "Mr. Judson!" she squealed.

"Sorry, Olivia," he said with a smile. "I just came to see Darcy home. It's pretty dark even with the moon out. Do you have your car?"

"Yes," Olivia said. "I could drive Darcy home."

"Thank you, but I have just a few more things to discuss with her." He fished a piece of paper from his pocket. "More catering business," he said. And then he waited.

Olivia got the picture. She said a hasty goodbye and then left.

For long seconds Darcy sat there staring at Patrick as he paced. His long legs made short work of the big kitchen. He scrubbed one hand through his hair. Finally he turned in a rush.

"Olivia told you what the girls said?"

Okay, more acting. "Yes, but don't worry. I don't see what the problem is."

He raised one eyebrow, an incredibly sexy move in Darcy's opinion. "Because?"

"Patrick, I understand that your sisters are worried about you, so I'm not offended that they would be looking out for your best interests, but no, there's no problem. You and I…well, all right, yes, I do find you attractive, but I'm not interested in dating you."

"Because I'm not on your list of men to date. I take it there *is* a list, then?"

Man, had she really said that? How was she going to get out of this?

"Every woman has a list, even if it's not a conscious one." She tried to affect a teasing tone.

"And who tops yours?"

Uh-oh. What could she say? Darcy's mind raced.

"It changes. I met a really nice man in my ballroom dancing class. Jared O'Donahue. He's a former cop."

"But you told me you weren't interested in a relationship."

She wasn't. Really, she didn't want to be. She couldn't. "Who said anything about a relationship? He's just an interesting man I'd like to get to know." She wasn't exactly lying here. Jared O'Donohue was a nice man, and they shared common interests and a common background. Like Patrick and Angelise. The very thought hardened her resolve. "I'm not sure where it's going, but yes, right now he tops my list." Especially since she had just started the list five seconds ago and Jared was the only man she could think of to put on it.

Patrick was studying her intently. "Be careful," he finally said.

She nodded, regret for things that could never be pummeling her heart. She so didn't want to be having this conversation. "Your Angelise is very beautiful. Are the two of you going to marry?"

"I'll eventually marry," he said, "but I don't intend to start looking until this tour is over."

"Of course. You'll be busy, and you'll want to play the field. Maybe you'll start your own list," she said with as bright a smile as she could manage.

For several seconds he simply stared at her, his green eyes

dark and intense. She thought of him staring into Angelise's eyes. And pain that she couldn't reveal filled her soul. Then he shook his head slowly. "I've never been interested in making lists," he said. "I prefer action."

And with that he moved forward. He scooped her right out of her chair and up against his chest. His lips came down on hers, searing her, claiming her, turning her mind to a mess of sheer desire. Automatically her hands threaded into his hair. She pressed closer, kissed back.

Heat swirled through her. Need conquered common sense. She hadn't even known that she needed this, but she did. Now that she'd tasted him this deeply, how could she ever not want to taste him every morning?

But she couldn't. The truths his sisters had spoken added to her own unspoken truths, the walls she'd built so carefully, her fears of what could go wrong if…

Darcy gave a muffled cry and pulled back. "This is so…no, I cannot do this," she said. "Put me down."

Patrick pulled back, far enough so that he could stare directly into her eyes. "Darcy, I—damn, I'm such a jerk. I apologize."

That made her mad. "Do *not* apologize. Just because I said I couldn't doesn't mean I didn't like it."

Now, he grinned. He carefully lowered her into her chair, his arms spanning her, his hands coming to rest on her tires as he gently trapped her.

"Next time I'll ask before I touch you," he said.

Darcy sucked in a deep breath. "Next time? You intend for there to be a next time?"

Patrick shrugged. "You told me that I wasn't on your list of men to date, but you didn't say I wasn't on your list of men to kiss. In fact, I distinctly heard you tell Olivia that I was on your top—"

She reached out and placed her fingers over his mouth.

"All right, you're hot," she conceded. "But we're not going to kiss again."

CHAPTER SEVEN

PATRICK was not a man to use his fists, but right now he wanted to hit something very hard. Had he actually asked her who she wanted to date, he asked himself hours after he'd taken her home? Had he taken her in his arms and kissed her? Had he, in other words, crossed several lines he shouldn't have even thought of crossing?

No question about it, he had, and he wasn't at all happy with himself.

She'd met a man, she had said. Jared O'Donohue. Was he a good man? The right man? Darcy had said that she'd been hurt when her fiancé had abandoned after her accident. And now?

"None of your business, Judson," he muttered beneath his breath. Nonetheless, he sat down at his computer and began to work. It didn't take long to come up with a smattering of information. Jared O'Donahue. Good-looking guy, twenty-seven years old, he'd been given awards for heroism and bravery, but had had his legs crushed when a vehicle had run into him and pinned him against his squad car. He was, from all accounts, the best type of man and if the man had a heart beating in his body and any consciousness of what made a woman desirable, he would be interested in Darcy.

Who could blame him?

What's more, the man had a lot in common with Darcy. Background, upbringing, even the accident and the chair. He would understand everything she thought and felt in a way Patrick never really could.

So…she'd met someone. That was a good thing, wasn't it? Wasn't it his goal to make sure that all the residents of Able House were happy and healthy? Being in a good relationship would certainly contribute to Darcy's happiness.

"Of course, it's a darned good thing," he said to the walls. So, why did he feel as if he'd missed something, lost something?

That couldn't matter. It was selfish, and he couldn't afford to be selfish where Darcy was concerned. That kind of attitude would end up hurting her. It wasn't going to happen.

Darcy woke up the next morning and realized that she'd been dreaming about being held in Patrick's arms. She'd been kissing him, and…then he had pulled her closer, twisting so that she ended up beneath him and he was smiling into her eyes, bracing himself above her.

"Kiss me, Darcy," he'd said, and she had, betraying her good intentions in her dreams. She'd reached out, and her palms had slid over the smooth, warm muscles of his chest. No cloth barring her way. He had been warm, hard, exciting. The pads of her fingertips had tingled, and—

They'd been in bed together.

Darcy groaned as she realized just how vivid her dream had been. She reached out and pulled a pillow over her head, but that didn't erase the vision or the bereft sensation she felt now that the dream had ended and reality had set in.

Dreaming about making love with Patrick? No wonder his

sisters were concerned. She was acting like a fool. Just because he had kissed her a couple of times.

He'd probably kissed a thousand women. And walked away from every one.

Except for maybe Angelise, Darcy thought, remembering the statuesque brunette with perfect breasts, a tanned, fit body and killer legs made even more gorgeous by the lacy stilettos she'd been wearing.

"Stop it," she muttered from beneath her pillow just as she realized that someone was knocking on her door.

Immediately she sat up, shrugged on a robe, transferred herself into her chair and rolled over to slide the pocket door open.

"How was it?" Cerise asked before the door had completed its slide. "You came home so late that I didn't get a chance to ask. Did Patrick walk you home?"

He had. And as he had seen her into the house, he had slid his palm over her cheek and thanked her once again in that low, deep voice that had seemed incredibly intimate in the darkness.

Where in the world was her pillow? She had to stop the images, the memories, the longings.

Yeah, that would really decrease Cerise's curiosity. Darcy took a deep breath and managed a composed smile. "It was very successful. The meal went well, and I had people asking me to cater their parties."

"Wow, I'm impressed, but how does Patrick feel about that?"

And just like that, it hit Darcy full force. "Patrick will be flying overseas in a few weeks. He'll be gone a long time and he won't be needing my services after that."

And when he returned, Darcy thought, would he marry the beautiful Angelise and settle down to have babies? Darcy's breath caught, her throat burned. How foolish she was to have had those fantasy dreams of him. Their worlds and their lives were so different…

She clenched her hands on the wheels of her chair as if to remind herself of that.

"Did you hear that Julio's company laid him off yesterday?" Cerise asked, changing the subject.

Immediately, indignation and regret shot through Darcy. Not Julio. That was so unfair. Julio was a favorite of everyone at Able House. He had been much older than the rest of them when he'd suffered his injury and his recovery had taken longer, so just getting back into life had been more difficult. His injury had been no impediment to his job as a midlevel executive at an insurance firm and for the past few years he'd returned to his old field. But he was already in his fifties and it would be difficult to face having to start over again. Getting a new job at his age would be a challenge.

"Did you hear what I said, Darce?"

Darcy blinked. "I'm sorry. I missed the last part."

"Patrick found him a job as an apprentice piano tuner. Julio is in love with the idea!"

"A piano tuner?"

"Sure. You know how he loves to play that baby grand in the lobby."

"Yes, but…"

"Apparently Patrick noticed his skill, questioned him about it and when he heard about the problem yesterday, he made some calls, pulled some strings and now Julio is over the top. He hated the insurance business."

And who else but Patrick would have even thought to notice or to put two and two together and come up with such a perfect solution? Patrick's attentiveness to detail, the care he took with all of them made Darcy's heart fill. And break.

Patrick was the kind of man every woman wanted to know. But could a woman know this much of him and not want to know more? But to open up that way to a man who was determined to leave…could she survive the heartbreak when he left her behind?

"Still," Cerise said. "All is not well." She related her concerns to Darcy. One of the other residents had had a run-in with one of the few neighbors who continued to resent having so many wheelchairs cruising around the elite neighborhood and, supposedly, negatively impacting their property values. Words had been exchanged. There had nearly been blows. It had been ugly.

Darcy frowned. "Don't tell Patrick," she said. "And tell everyone else to keep it a secret from him, too. Patrick will only worry, and this is something he can't fix. He can't change every person's opinion of us, and I don't want him to leave here concerned that things aren't right for the residents of Able House. If he's concerned…"

She didn't want to be a responsibility to him, a loose end he hadn't tied up. Darcy bit her lip.

"Darce?"

Darcy looked at her friend. "I'll spread the word," Cerise promised. "Are we still going dancing tonight? You said we'd hit the Domenici Ballroom out in the suburbs. I assume Jared will be there?"

Jared? Darcy had almost forgotten about him. That wasn't right at all. Jared was the man she should be thinking about. They had a lot in common. He was a nice man, a handsome man. For sure, she would try to start thinking of him romantically, but for now…

"We're going," she agreed. "We'll talk more later. I have to get ready for work now."

I have to get ready to steel myself not to think about kissing Patrick when I see him this morning, she thought.

But later, when she finished setting up the small buffet she had arranged for breakfast and Patrick, the only early riser in the house, came up behind her, she turned and the first thing she looked at was his lips. And those arms that had held her, those hands that had touched her...

She caught herself and frowned.

"Don't," he said just as if she had spoken. "I'm not going to touch you again if you don't want me to."

She wanted him to. "It wouldn't be a good idea," she told him. Or was it herself she was reminding?

Darcy started to retreat to the kitchen.

"Could I have a minute of your time?" he asked.

She stopped moving and waited.

Patrick sat down in a chair beside her. "In two days time, I'm supposed to be helping out at a fund-raiser for a children's charity. It was organized before you started working for me, and since it's a brief affair, food wasn't to be a part of it. But Eleanor, who's also involved, apparently had one of those middle-of-the-night aha! moments. She asked if I could convince you to prepare some treats for the kids, but I don't want you to feel obligated in any way. I know that's not in your job description."

She looked at Patrick and saw that he was studying her intently. That dark green gaze seemed to see parts of her soul that she had been trying very hard to keep hidden.

"This is an event where there will be lots of children," he said, his voice deep and low and gentle. "And...your aversion to my nephews at dinner was more than simple dislike, wasn't it?" he asked.

Indignation and remorse threatened to overwhelm her. "I

didn't dislike them! I couldn't. They're adorable. Sweet. So very little and innocent, but…"

Patrick waited.

"It's not that simple," she finally said. "Remember how I told you that I was engaged when I had my accident?"

"Of course. Your fiancé turned out to be a shallow imbecile."

She managed a slightly wobbly smile. "Thank you, but there's more. I wasn't just engaged. I was pregnant. I lost my baby."

He leaned toward her. "Darcy…"

She held up one hand. "I'm not telling you this so that you'll feel sorry for me, but so that you'll understand. I could never dislike your nephews. I just can't—"

As if he didn't even see her hand, Patrick reached out. "Darcy," he said again, pulling her onto his lap and tucking her against him. "I'm so sorry you lost your child."

Darcy felt warm and safe lying here against Patrick's heart. She felt as if she could tell him anything. "It wasn't just the loss of my baby that made me this way," she said. "Under other circumstances, I think I might have healed a bit more than I have or maybe even tried again. As it was, not long after I finished my physical therapy when I was first learning to get around in the chair, I was in a shopping center where I'd gone to practice maneuvering. As I was moving past a flight of stairs, I looked up. Back in those days I always looked up when I saw stairs. The newness and the despair of realizing that staircases had become as insurmountable as a snow-capped Mount Everest seemed to draw my attention every time. But this time, it wasn't just the stairs. There was a little girl, a toddler standing at the top of the staircase, playing. Her mother must have moved away or looked away for a minute, and the child…she was so close to the edge and she was ungainly in the way children of that age are.

"In my mind, I can still see her taking one more step and I can still feel the horror that there was no way I could even begin to try to help her in time. I yelled, but I didn't think anyone heard. The little girl pitched forward and...just as she did, someone, another woman shot past me and caught her. She'd fallen a step or two and was banged up a bit, but she hadn't tumbled very far. I was so relieved, but also...so scared. I kept thinking, what if that person hadn't passed by at that moment? And what if I ever had a child? I couldn't chase her in that kind of a situation. I might not be able to move fast enough or to reach her if she was somewhere that my chair wouldn't go and...I just can't have children," she finished quietly, looking up at Patrick. "I can't—I don't want to be too near children. It's just so painful. The fear is always there. The loss is always there, because I wanted them...so much."

"Shh, Darcy, Darcy," Patrick said, rocking her in his arms. "I promise you I won't put you through that. I won't—I'm calling Eleanor and telling her no."

Instantly Darcy sat up. "No, that's not what I meant. You'll do no such thing."

Patrick looked startled.

"I mean...don't call Eleanor, please," Darcy said, realizing that she had, once again, forgotten that Patrick was her boss. She quickly pushed away from him and transferred herself to her chair. "I can't be *with* them, but...preparing the food...that is one thing I *can* do for a child. I can be anonymous but still give something. It's such a small thing, but it would mean a lot to me. Please let me help in this one little way," she said.

He shook his head.

Darcy frowned. "Why not? Are you telling me no?"

"I'm telling you yes. I'm telling you that you're an amazing woman, Darcy Parrish."

But she couldn't allow herself to accept compliments from him, not when she felt herself to be a coward. Had she really been so far gone that she had allowed him to take her onto his lap? She could have said no. She was sure he would have listened to her. That was the kind of man he was.

Instead she had snuggled up to him and fallen even farther into infatuation.

"Hey, this isn't such a big deal. It will be fun for me," she said, knowing that it would be a form of torture, of penance for not being more mentally tough. And staying here with Patrick any longer was only going to test her resolve to back away from what she was beginning to feel for him.

"I'd better go think of something to make." She turned away.

"Thank you. I have to get going, anyway. I'm on my way over to Able House."

Uh-oh. Her mind went on full-alert. "Something wrong?" Had he heard about the new argument with the neighbor and the heated words that had been exchanged?

"No, not at all. Just details. Eric is moving to Tennessee, but I guess you knew that."

"Oh. Sure." She smiled brightly. Maybe too brightly.

"Something wrong?" he asked, using her own words.

"No. Nothing." Darn. Definitely too bright. She'd been caught off guard with no time to don her poker face.

Patrick leaned close. He bent down. "Okay, you don't want to share?" he whispered near her ear, sending a thrill through her body. "I won't pry into your secrets."

That was good, because her darkest secret was that while she had promised herself she wouldn't be interested in Patrick, she was. She wanted to feast on his kisses.

Thank goodness she was going dancing with Jared tonight. Surely if she paid more attention to him, common sense would kick in, she would develop an attraction to Jared, their friendship might turn into something more, and this insane something she was feeling for Patrick would completely disappear.

Maybe she'd even be on the road to being over him by tonight.

CHAPTER EIGHT

PATRICK lay awake in the gathering light the next morning and cursed the reason why he had tossed and turned all last night. When he'd gone to Able House yesterday, Cerise, who taught fitness classes, had been the only resident around and she'd practically been bouncing around in her chair.

"You look happy," Patrick had told her, and she had explained to him that she and Darcy were going dancing later that evening with some friends. It had been clear from the glow in her eyes that the friends were men.

The cop, he had thought. Be happy for Darcy, he'd told himself.

He was. He was also something else, something unacceptable, and he didn't want to think about that. He had no business being jealous of Jared O'Donahue just because the man had spent the evening dancing with Darcy. And yet…

Patrick let out a growl, got out of bed and stood under a cold shower. Then, he went to the kitchen and prowled around. Darcy wasn't there, but Lane was.

"Where is she?" he asked.

Lane didn't even bother pretending she didn't know. "Cara and Amy are coming over. I wanted to have breakfast on the lawn, so I had your new gardener carry the tables and gear out. Darcy is out there with a blender and some secret ingredients making something luscious, fruity and frothy for us to drink."

Patrick nodded. He made a beeline for the French doors and continued on a straight line until he reached the semi-shaded area at the far end of the broad expanse of lawn where Darcy was working her magic.

She stopped her blender at his approach. "Bad night?" she asked. "You look grumpy."

"You're not supposed to tell your boss he looks grumpy," he said.

She peeked up at him from beneath those long eyelashes, a mischievous look on her face. "Too late. I already did."

"You seem very lively this morning. Have a good evening?" Patrick cursed himself for not being able to prevent himself from asking the question. Dammit, her private life was none of his business, was it?

Her wonderfully expressive face had grown more pensive at his question. Slightly distressed.

"Forget I asked that. Cerise told me that you were going dancing, but I shouldn't be intruding on your privacy."

"No, it's all right. Really." She waved her hand, dismissing his concern. It's just, I should have had a good time. I've loved the lessons so far. The dancing is exciting and fun and I love learning new things, but up until now the lessons have been private. Last night, at a public ballroom where we stood out so much, I felt as if I was on display. It was a small crowd, so it wasn't completely terrible, but…it was uncomfortable. I felt as if we were taking up too much space on the dance floor."

"You had as much right to be there as everyone else."

Darcy laughed suddenly, a bright sound. "Thank you for

saying that, but…I wish you could see your face. You look so wonderfully miffed on my behalf. A little bit pompous, too, as only someone of your stature can be."

Patrick couldn't help himself then. "As if you care about my stature." And wasn't that part of Darcy's appeal? She didn't care about his rank. She didn't care about…

He stopped himself cold. He'd been nearing forbidden territory again. "Was Jared there, then?" he asked, wading right in where he didn't want to go.

"Who's Jared?" Cara's voice broke into his thoughts and Patrick turned to see his sister marching across the lawn, toddler in hand.

He felt the lightness fade right out of Darcy even though he couldn't see her. Panic, sadness emanated from her. He could sense it. And—was it his imagination or did she retreat further behind the table?

"Jared is a friend of Darcy's," he said. "And none of our business."

"Oh? Sounds delicious," Amy said, following her sister. "I'm happy for you, Darcy." She sounded happy, too. Too happy.

Patrick shot her a warning look. He quickly scooped up Charlie on one arm and Davey on the other as if to protect Darcy, even though his nephews were loving little boys. "Hey, scamp," he said to Charlie.

"Me, too?" Davey said.

"Absolutely, you, too. I was just going to say hi, scoot," he told Davey. The little boy beamed.

Patrick felt Darcy's eyes on him and turned to catch a look of such pained longing, such utter sadness that he quickly made his excuses and started to carry the boys away.

"You haven't had your breakfast," Darcy said, but her voice seemed a bit broken.

"It's all right, Darcy," he said, even though it was clear that nothing was all right. "I'm fine."

She got a stubborn look in her pretty eyes. "Breakfast is the most important meal of the day. You shouldn't miss it."

Amy's and Cara's eyebrows rose.

"I know. I have a bad habit of lecturing him. I'm working on it," she told his sisters, that stubborn, unbending look still firming up that pretty chin of hers.

"I wouldn't worry about trying to learn not to lecture him," Lane said as she came outside, too. "After all, he's leaving the country soon. Then how you treat him will be a moot point since he won't even be around. By the time he comes back, who knows? He might be married and have a wife who cooks for him and lectures him."

"Lane," Patrick said sternly. It was totally clear that his sister was warning Darcy off, even though he knew that Darcy didn't need any warning because she wasn't interested.

"I didn't mean that you would leave Darcy high and dry," his youngest sister reasoned. "Because, of course, she'll go directly from here right to another job, right?"

He didn't answer at first. It occurred to him how quickly time was flying by.

Amy and Cara came closer. Patrick noticed that Lane was tugging at a strand of hair. It was an old habit and a sure sign of a guilty conscience. "I mean, you'll make sure Darcy has a good place to go, won't you, Patrick?" she asked.

"Because you always taught us that we needed to care for our employees' feelings," Cara cut in.

"And we know that you've already found at least temporary jobs for everyone else who'll be left with nothing to do when you're gone," Amy added.

"Darcy, I apologize," Lane said. "Those things I said—that

was mean of me and…not okay. I didn't mean to be so flippant. But I naturally thought that Patrick would—"

"She'll have the best," Patrick finally said. "I promise you that. I look after my own." But, of course, she wasn't his own, he thought as he carried his nephews into the house, fed them there and kept them there. He didn't want to leave Darcy alone with his sisters, but he couldn't bear to see how torn up she was when the boys were around.

His sisters did have a way of blurting out whatever was on their minds. Almost as much as Darcy did.

Maybe he should have asked them to find out if she was falling in love with Jared.

But maybe he didn't actually want to know that.

"These muffins are decadent, Darcy," Amy told her. "I—I apologize, too. We've been rude. Thoughtless. It's just that…"

Darcy turned to face Patrick's middle sister. "Thank you for the compliment. And don't worry. I know you're concerned that I might have some sort of crush on Patrick, but that's not going to be a problem."

Amy blushed.

Cara rushed forward. "What Amy meant was, yes, we're concerned about Patrick, but not in the way you think. He gave up so much for us and never, ever made us feel that he was sacrificing his happiness, not even when he got called home from the prom because one of us had gotten in trouble. But we knew he had to want more. Now he can have more, but…we're also worried that without at least one of us to fuss over, he'll be lonely. And we have female friends—not just Angelise, but others, too, who've been waiting for the chance to date Patrick. We've been making plans and—"

And. Cara didn't have to say more. Darcy Parrish hadn't

been in the plans. She almost wanted to laugh. Wasn't that just the very thing that had tripped her up all her life? Either she hadn't been in someone else's plans and had messed with their situation, or life had thrown her a curve that hadn't been in her plans. But that had to change. She didn't want to be remembered as a negative in Patrick's life, someone who showed up at the wrong time and messed things up for him and kept him from meeting the perfect woman.

Heaven knew she wasn't the perfect woman, and by perfect Darcy wasn't thinking about her legs. She was thinking about those two little boys and how right they had looked snuggled up in Patrick's arms, how he should have some children of his own to cuddle and spoil and raise and love. Her heart hurt at the thought.

Slowly she shook her head. "You don't have to worry. I'm not going to have a romantic entanglement with your brother," she said quietly.

The three of them nodded, though guilt still seemed to register in their eyes. They ate their breakfast in silence, then picked up their plates, said a subdued goodbye to Darcy and walked toward the house. As they neared the graceful white building, Darcy thought she heard them rattling off names of women.

Five minutes later, Patrick came out to where she was cleaning up the area. "I was just going to call Peter to help me get all this inside," she said.

"Will I do, instead?"

She looked up into those compelling green eyes. Yes, he would do, a small, wistful voice inside her shouted. He was the kind of man that every girl dreamed of, wasn't he? Even smart-mouthed girls from the wrong side of the tracks who couldn't possibly ever have someone like this?

"I don't know," she said, pasting on a grin to lighten the mood and hide her wistfulness. "Let me see your muscles."

Patrick raised a brow. He turned and struck a mocking pose. It was meant to be silly, but oh, he did have a fantastic set of muscles.

"Okay, I think you can handle a few utensils. At least light ones," she teased, hoping she didn't sound breathless.

"Yes, but the question is can I handle you?" he asked as they gathered some of the gear and headed toward the house.

"Handle me?" Darcy hoped she didn't sound breathless.

"Able House. What's going on there? I meant to talk to you earlier but I didn't want to have this conversation in front of my sisters. The thing is that when I showed up at Able House yesterday I could tell that something was wrong. People kept looking at me and whispering, but when I asked them to tell me what was happening, no one would say anything. Eventually I heard someone whisper your name, but by then I knew trying to get information from them wasn't going to work. So, I'm taking my questions straight to the source. What's going on with you, Darcy?" They had entered the house and he had put the things he'd been carrying down. He leaned closer.

She stopped breathing. What was going on with her? Him. This. This ridiculous, silly, unacceptable longing she felt whenever he got too close. After she'd just told his sisters—

"Nothing's going on with me," she said solemnly. And she meant it. She willed it to be true.

"Then what's wrong at Able House?"

Darcy considered ignoring the question or lying, but now that he had asked her directly...

"Tell me," he said, his voice a rough whisper. "I can help. I'll try to help."

"No, you can't, Patrick. You can't fix everything for us. You've done so much, but…"

Darcy flung her arm out. "You can't make everything right for us. All of us know that. Some battles can't be won. We know it. We live it, and…we're so incredibly grateful to you for what you're doing, but…"

"I don't want your gratitude," he said, his voice low and dark and husky.

"But you have it," she told him. "I can't stop that."

He was close now. So very close.

"I hate it that someone might have wronged you in a neighborhood where I set you up."

"It's just one or two people."

"But it wouldn't have happened somewhere else."

"You don't know that."

"I think I do. I've lived here all my life. There are always a few people who don't like young children or dogs that don't have pure enough bloodlines or—"

He didn't have to finish. There were two neighbors who just weren't happy about Able House and probably never would be.

"I'll talk to them again," he said. And he would come away frustrated and feeling guilty, because Darcy knew the kind of person they were dealing with. She'd dealt with them in that school and on her job from time to time. She'd seen the lack of acceptance in her former fiancé's expression.

"Don't do it," she said, reaching out to catch Patrick's wrist. "It just isn't worth it."

"Darcy."

"Promise me," she said.

He stared into her eyes for so long that she was afraid she would lean toward him, signal him, show him how drawn to him she was.

Instead he looked down to where she clasped his wrist. He covered her hand with his, turning her hand so that her palm was up. Then he brought her hand to his lips and kissed that most sensitive center of her palm.

Desire shot through her so fast she couldn't contain it.

He kissed her palm again, his lips soft and warm.

"Don't let me do more than this," he said. "I want to kiss you, but if you tell me no, I won't."

Darcy sat there just a breath away from Patrick. He had replaced his lips with his thumb and was tracing long, slow circles on her skin. She could barely sit still, could barely keep from moaning.

When more seconds than she could count had passed and she still hadn't spoken, he turned to her, leaned toward her. His lips were close. If she leaned forward just slightly, she would be against him. She could kiss him, feel him, feel right.

"Tell me no," he told her again.

She reached up and threaded her fingers through his hair. "No," she said, even as she pulled him down to her and touched her lips to his.

She kissed him greedily, tasted him, savored him.

He didn't touch her. Only a low growl escaped him, but his body was rigid, hot, tense.

Darcy kissed him again. She wanted more. She wanted… she wanted…

"Please," she said. "Please, yes. Just one kiss."

"Thank you," he said on a groan and pulled her to him. He dropped to his knees so that he was slightly below her and he nuzzled his mouth against hers. Then he covered her more fully, licking at the seam of her mouth, exploring her carefully, hotly. He was making her insane.

He cupped her face in his palms and replaced his lips with

his thumb, discovering the shape of her mouth, making her shiver with his light, teasing touch. His hand drifted lower, to her chin, her throat. Wherever he touched, he followed up with a trail of kisses that left her aching for more.

"I—Patrick—I—"

"I love the way the scent of cinnamon and vanilla clings to your skin. I want to breathe you in. Deeply. You make me want things," he whispered against her skin. "Things I didn't even know I wanted before. And I know I should stay away. I want to stay away, but—"

As he spoke, his lips continued on their fiery path until his mouth was against that oh-so-sensitive line where her injury had occurred, where sensation was always more intense, a line of demarcation that—

Patrick kissed her there and Darcy's mind went blank, then turned hot, needy and—

Oh, he'd just said that he wanted to stay away. She'd just promised his sisters that she wouldn't do this, want this, be this way and yet…

Patrick kissed her, his touch shaking her to the core.

His sisters would bring other women. Angelise. More. He would do this with them, too, she thought and knew that it was true.

Something broke inside her. Something hurt. What was she doing? "No more."

Her voice barely ranked as a whisper, the sound was so soft, but Patrick stopped. Immediately. He was breathing hard, his green eyes were glazed with desire so heated that Darcy could barely look for fear she'd reach out and grab him again, but he stopped. Completely.

"We can't," she said, biting at her lip. "I'm sorry. I keep doing this, but—I have to be whole when this is over. So do you. And you—I—this might leave a scar, unfinished business. I don't want any unfinished business in my life. It's more than I can handle."

Slowly he nodded. He reached out and gently righted her clothes, even though she hadn't registered till now just how disheveled she was.

"I'll try not to let this happen again," he said, "but you must know by now that you have a tendency to make me lose my self-control."

"You might have noticed that I was the one who grabbed you."

"But you didn't want to."

"No."

"As I said, I'll try to make sure it doesn't happen again." Just as if he could control the whole thing. And maybe he could. He'd been put in charge of the care and feeding and rearing of three sisters when he'd only been nineteen. Control had been a part of his life for so many years.

And wasn't that part of what his trip was about? Do some good, do some business and let loose of all that stunning control?

Yet, here he was, promising her that he would take care of things once again. He would police himself and her as well. And he would take the blame if anything went awry.

His sisters were right. Entirely right. He needed lightness and fun and a woman who wasn't going to always be making him feel the heavy responsibility of maintaining control. With the right kind of woman, he could let loose. He could give one hundred percent and he could be happy.

"You don't have to make sure it won't happen. I'll do that," she said.

He had risen and the quick frown he cast her way, the rigid line of his jaw, didn't bode well for her power grab. She needed a distraction, a change of topic.

"Got to go."

"We're not done yet, Darcy. Things aren't settled."

"Yes. They are. And I have to figure out what treat I'm making for that benefit for the children tomorrow. No time to waste. I've got lots of work to do. Things to decide. Supplies to purchase."

He let her flutter a bit. Then he stared her down until she stopped.

"It wasn't a whim," he told her. "Not something I do lightly. I want you to know that."

She didn't want to know that. She didn't want to think about it. Thinking meant longing, and longing meant admitting that he was just one more thing she couldn't have. No, not that. Not *just*. He was so much more than just one more thing. He was major.

"If things were different. If I weren't your benefactor and if—"

Darcy let out a small, fierce cry. She reached up as if to press her fingertips over his lips. No, she so didn't want to hear that. If things were different and they tried to make this something more than it could ever be, then…

I'd be another responsibility to him, she thought. He would never have that carefree time he craved and needed. He would never have that easy fling with a woman, because much as she liked herself, Darcy knew that nothing about her was easy.

"Things aren't different," she said carefully, trying not to look too deeply into his eyes. Then, as quickly as she could go, she escaped.

A part of her wished that he would follow her, but he didn't. And she knew that it was for the best. Sometimes doing the right thing felt…wrong. This business of training herself not to want Patrick's touch was going to take some time.

* * *

The next time Darcy saw Patrick was the next day when he came to load his van and take her to the fund-raiser.

"Have you spoken to Eleanor?" she asked, trying for some light conversation.

"Yes. An hour ago."

"Oh, things must be taking off, then."

"Yes, I think so. She did tell me to let you know that a few more children than she had originally told you about had been added."

Was that an evasive look on his face?

"Oh," she said. "How many more will there be?"

For a second Patrick looked uncomfortable. "Let's just say that Eleanor was a bit distraught and Eleanor is pretty much unflappable."

Darcy felt panic creeping through her chest. "So…how many exactly did you say?"

"I didn't."

"I know. Patrick," she drawled, trying to look stern.

"Let's just say…too many."

The panic grew. She gave him an exasperated look. "Let's just be really exact. I need to know if I have enough supplies and if I made enough to go around."

Patrick swore beneath his breath. "All right. I was trying to save you from panic. Fifty more."

Fifty? There had already been two hundred on the original list, and—

"Okay. All right. I can handle that many," Darcy said, trying to convince herself. "I'm not panicking."

Liar. Panic was beating at her like a bird's frantic wings. It was speeding up, taking over. *What was she going to do about that?*

"Okay, let's see. Well, fifty more? Hmm, Patrick, I'm definitely going to go throw up now. You might not want to stick around for this. I can guarantee that it won't be pretty."

And just like that, he was on his knees in front of her, smiling up into her face. "I'll help you," he said. "I'll stay beside you all the way. You're going to be so great. They'll absolutely love you."

"You're a very brave man kneeling in front of a woman who just told you she was going to be sick."

"Well, what can I tell you?" he asked with a wink as he rose. "I'm a risk-taker."

He was. She knew that. She knew about the skateboarding and the bungee jumping and the skydiving. He loved the challenge.

And she was not a risk-taker. She might have a smart mouth, but that was all a self-defense move, a mask to hide behind. She admitted it, and Patrick probably knew it as well.

He also knew something else. He knew how to distract a woman perfectly. She was no longer feeling sick or worrying about how she was going to come through for two hundred fifty children.

Instead she was worrying about how she was going to manage to get through the afternoon. Patrick had said he was going to be beside her the whole way.

Darcy pressed her palms over her chest and concentrated on breathing in and out. And she began to count to two hundred fifty. By the time she reached that magic number, she was hoping common sense would have returned and her panic would have subsided.

There was, after all, nothing to worry about. This was a totally public event. She wasn't going to drag Patrick down and kiss him again. What could possibly happen?

CHAPTER NINE

DARCY was amazing, Patrick thought, watching her at work. The fund-raiser was in a big, beautiful new building and she was closed up in the kitchen, secluded from the area where hundreds of children had gathered. Eleanor had been more than willing to transfer this to a venue with an open-air kitchen so everyone could watch Darcy work her magic. Instead this place was totally utilitarian and sterile, and probably most people would have found the setup a bit boring. Demanding. Not at all fun or energizing. But Darcy was glowing.

Just an hour earlier, the countertops had been groaning beneath the weight of what had seemed like thousands of finger sandwiches decorated with colorful cream cheese frostings, various pitchers of pink and green and blue smoothies and fruit cups topped off with whipped cream and star sprinkles. There had been home-baked potato chips and a dinosaur centerpiece surrounded by a wall of cheese cubes.

"So, what do you think?" she asked him, holding out a tray of cookies shaped like cars and airplanes, unicorns and stars and various other shapes. Each cookie had a child's name swirled on in a contrasting color.

"I think you must be totally insane," he told her. "Insane, but very cute with that frosting on your nose." He gently wiped it off with an index finger, then licked his finger.

Bad mistake. She blushed, and he felt heat swirl through him. He ignored it. "Two hundred fifty individualized cookies, Darcy?"

"Well, all of them but the last fifty were made in advance. I had Eleanor give me a list of names. Olivia was there to help me with the first two hundred, and, as you know, she was here earlier until she had to leave."

He knew. He had positioned himself at the door to make sure that no one intruded, so she could have the privacy she needed, and be out of sight of the children whose presence clearly brought her pain. Now, the event was almost over except for the finale, those amazing cookies she'd whipped up and tirelessly decorated.

Patrick signaled the last of the students he'd hired to go ahead and distribute the cookies. Then, he looked around at the kitchen. It was almost immaculate, even though he'd watched Darcy destroy the place during her preparations. The food and the kids, not the state of the hospital white kitchen had clearly been her priorities, but now she and her crew had worked a miracle cleanup worthy of a magician.

"Almost done," she told him as she took a few last swipes at a table with a damp cloth. "We can leave soon." But, he saw her gaze shift toward the door where children's voices suddenly rose higher. Obviously Eleanor had planned some sort of exciting grand finale.

"Are you sure you don't want to go have a look?" he asked.

She gave him a wary, tired and very tight smile. "No, I'm okay right here. Do you think they liked the food? Not that kids pay that much attention to food, I know, but…"

"Darcy," he said, cutting in. "You made every item so kid friendly that they would have had to be asleep not to have loved it. In fact, I saw two munchkins comparing those cream cheese faces you had put on their sandwiches. I think they were striking a deal, a trade, and both of them looked immensely pleased with themselves." Which was, in fact, the truth.

"Good. Eleanor told me that some of them end up eating the same thing every day because they can't afford anything but the least expensive items. I remember what it was like not to have variety. Oh well, let me just finish putting away one or two more things."

He nodded, just as a voice sounded behind him. He turned to tell the person approaching that this room was a private area, but before he could do that, a woman with a camera came barreling past him. She flashed a badge dangling from her neck, some sort of press ID or something, but she kept moving, making a beeline for Darcy.

"Suburban Gazette," she said. "Just a few quick questions, Ms. Parrish. You *are* Ms. Parrish, aren't you? The one who did the catering?"

Without asking, she stuck her camera into Darcy's face and clicked off several rapid shots.

Patrick didn't even hesitate. He stepped between Darcy and the woman. "She's off-limits," he said.

Darcy's groan was almost imperceptible, but he heard it and knew what she was thinking. She was right. He should have known better. His statement had just made Darcy much more interesting than she had been a moment before. A talented chef in a wheelchair was intriguing. One who had a bodyguard was doubly intriguing, and when that bodyguard was one of the wealthiest men in the city, well...

"What Mr. Judson meant was that I'm off-limits because I'm

in the midst of the creative process. We're planning his sister's surprise going-away-to-college party, but if word gets out…" Darcy blew out a frustrated sigh so big that her bangs lifted off her forehead. "We would just have to go back to square one and plan something else. There wouldn't even be any party," she said, pointedly staring at the reporter.

"So…I would be writing about a nonexistent event?" the woman said.

"Exactly."

"But you have to know that I don't care about the party. I came here to interview you."

"Another time, perhaps," Darcy said, pasting on an angelic smile that Patrick had never witnessed. "Ms.—I'm sorry, I don't know your name, and the print on your name tag is pretty small and above my line of sight and—well, it's hanging right over your…um, your chest."

"Ms. Compton," the woman said.

"Ms. Compton, you're a writer and a photographer, clearly a creative individual. Were you ever in the middle of creating something and had the process interrupted? I just—it's so— it's difficult to explain to someone who doesn't make their living using their imagination, but—"

The woman smiled. "Okay, you win. Interrupt the process and the best ideas may be lost in the ether and never return. I understand and…all right, I'll go." And she turned to do just that. Just before she left, she turned back. "Is it all right if I use the picture?"

Darcy's angelic smile disappeared. It was replaced with a look of anguish. "I really need people to know me for my talents, not for…other things," she said. "Would it be all right if you skipped the picture and just mentioned my name as the chef? I'm starting a catering business, and that would be a big help."

The woman considered the question. "The photo might bring in business."

"Not the kind I want. Let me put it this way…if this were an earlier era, would you want to be hired because you were a female reporter and, therefore, a curiosity or would you want to be courted for your talent?"

The woman considered that. "Okay, you win again. Just a one or two sentence mention of you and those great smoothies. I had one," she confessed. "I could live on those things."

And then she was gone.

Patrick sat down on a chair across from Darcy. "Are you okay?"

She nodded.

"I'm sorry," he said. "I nearly messed things up for you there."

Darcy shrugged. "I would have weathered the gossip."

As she had weathered the taunts of her old classmates and the desertion of her idiot of a fiancé and the loss of her baby.

"I'm supposed to be helping you engineer your success, not rocketing you into the tabloids."

Her mouth tipped up slightly. "The tabloids? Good thing Ms. Compton didn't hear you refer to her newspaper that way."

He grinned. "I wanted to say worse."

Darcy studied him, tilting her head. "Do you really end up in the tabloids?"

"Not usually. My life is too dull."

Her laugh was delicious. "How can it be dull when you have three sisters all trying to marry you off? I've seen the photos of all those gorgeous women Lane's been leaving on the breakfast table for you to chance upon, and I've heard about all those luscious women drooling over you."

But he didn't want just any woman drooling over him.

"Drooling isn't high on my list of admirable qualities in a wife."

She laughed. "What is?"

He stared at her. She blushed, then licked her lips nervously, making him want to groan, to snatch her up, to touch her, taste her, know all of her.

"Because," she rushed on, "maybe I could guide your sisters, point them in the right direction."

Anger rushed over Patrick. Darcy so clearly wasn't interested in him, not for the long-term, anyway.

"Do *not* start matchmaking with my sisters," he said, his voice rough and uneven. "I would hate that. You know I'm attracted to you." He got up and began to pace the room, shoving a hand through his hair. On his fourth trip back across the room, he noticed that she was holding a paper napkin that she was shredding, the pieces falling on her lap and to the floor.

Immediately he stopped pacing. "I'm being a total jerk. I'm sorry."

She looked up at him with those big, beautiful eyes. "Do you think I'm not attracted to you, too? You know I am, but I can't—this—this thing that keeps happening between us— it's just one of those benefactor, beneficiary situations. We're attracted because we're thrown together so much, it's…circumstantial, and it's not real. It's not—I don't want it."

"Shh, I'm sorry." He took the remains of the napkin from her and kissed her fingertips. "I'm sorry. What do you want?"

"I want to go home now, please."

"Absolutely. It's as good as done."

"And Patrick?"

He looked down into her eyes.

"I told that reporter I was planning a surprise party for Lane."

"I'm not putting more work on you. You're already

swamped with business. I saw Eleanor bringing you all those business cards and she told me that you were booking up fast. There will be a discreet notice placed in the newspaper that the Judsons dined privately for Lane's last day at home. The reporter will simply think that we've changed our plans."

As the last word fell from his lips, he realized that he had veered from his own plans. He'd been thinking about Darcy more than his trip lately, but she was right. This was circumstantial. She had things she wanted and needed, and he had dreams he'd wanted to pursue all his life. It was time to turn those dreams, hers and his, into reality.

In two weeks time, he intended to be in France, with Darcy a distant memory. But before that happened, he was going to take care of a few things for her.

He was going to create some opportunities. The fact that those opportunities would only create more of a chasm between them...well, that was a good thing, wasn't it?

Well, she had officially turned into a liar, Darcy thought, later that evening. She had said that she didn't want whatever it was that she felt pulsing between her and Patrick, and that was a flat-out lie. She wanted all of it. Every second.

And if she grabbled for it, then when he left...

A garbled moan escaped her lips.

"Something wrong?" Olivia asked.

"Nothing." Everything. Except...even though she'd been talking off the top of her head when she'd mentioned that benefactor, beneficiary concept, maybe, hopefully that *was* a big part of the attraction. Patrick was attracted to her because she was a novelty, and she was attracted to him because she owed him so much. He was a man who had been kind to her in ways she wasn't accustomed to.

Instantly an image of Jared came to mind. Jared had been kind. He was a friend.

She shook her head. This was different somehow.

"Darcy, what is going on with you? You're muttering and shaking your head," Olivia said.

"I've got lots of work. Just look at all these events Eleanor has snagged for me."

"You love work," Olivia pointed out.

Darcy gave her friend a deadpan look. "You're far too smart and intuitive for someone just out of high school."

"It doesn't take intuition to know that work makes you happy when you practically shriek every time you come up with a new way to serve artichokes or when you spend hours practicing your plating skills and go home with a grin on your face. Or the way you practically float on a cloud when Mr. Judson follows his nose to your coffee."

Okay, that was getting just too personal. But…

"I want to do something for Patrick before he leaves," she said.

"Kiss him?"

Darcy gave Olivia an evil glare. "That was not funny."

"But you know you want to. Everyone does."

"Not you."

"He's too old for me, and anyway, I have a boyfriend, but you…"

"I have Jared."

Olivia studied her friend. "Do you really feel that way about Jared?"

"What way?"

"Oh…like you daydream about kissing him, like you wonder what he looks like naked."

She had never even thought of Jared naked.

"How do you know I haven't *seen* him naked?"

"Have you?"

Darcy wrinkled her nose.

"I thought not," Olivia said. "You don't have 'the look' when he's around. When he came to pick you up to go dancing the other day, it was as if he was just the mailman delivering your mail."

"We have a nice mailman."

"Exactly. Your Jared is nice. But if I asked you about Mr. Judson, you wouldn't say that he was nice. Not in that way, anyway."

"What way would I say it?"

"Your voice would get all soft and kind of choked up, as if you were weak or something."

"I'm not weak."

"Weak? My Darcy? Never."

Darcy squealed and turned around. "Patrick!" she said, and her voice did, indeed, come out in a rather weak whisper. She cleared her throat and tried again. "You have got to stop doing that."

"Doing what?"

Being you, she wanted to say. Proving Olivia right.

"Sneaking up on me. At least stomp around a bit before you enter the kitchen. Or growl or shriek or something. Maybe a trumpet."

His laugh was warm and delicious and just the way a man's laugh should be.

"Sorry," he said with a wink. "I just…I needed to ask you something." He looked up at Olivia and Darcy knew he was going to ask Olivia to leave. Then she would be totally alone with him, and given the way she was feeling right now she didn't trust herself one bit. If she wasn't careful, she might do something terrible like think of him the way Olivia had suggested that she might. To Darcy's consternation, she noticed that Patrick's shirt was open at the neck, the sleeves of his white shirt were rolled up. He had the most wonderful arms, the most amazing hands. Her breathing kicked up.

"Olivia stays," she said.

He raised a brow.

"Please," she added.

"Olivia stays if you like. I just wanted to ask you if you would have any objections to Jared moving into Able House. There's an opening and the directors asked for my input. But your input is much more valuable and valid than mine. I know you like him. Would you want…"

He glanced at Olivia again.

"I'm out of here," she said, ignoring Darcy's panicked look.

"I wasn't sure what the situation is," he told Darcy. "I don't like interfering in your more personal affairs and this feels very much like interference."

What should she say? If she said yes…people already thought that Jared was romantically interested in her, and if she recommended him for this slot even Jared might begin to wonder if she was interested in *him*. Still, he was a friend, no matter what. Able House was an opportunity. Could she deny her friend this chance just because there might be complications she didn't want?

"Give the spot to Jared," she said.

He gave a tight nod. "It's done," he said, and he was gone just as quickly as he had arrived.

Darcy felt an urge to scream, to punch something. Patrick was putting up another barrier. That was a good thing. He was trying to do one more favor for her when he'd already done so many.

"This being a beneficiary all the time is making me insane," she said out loud.

So...turn the tables. Do something for Patrick. Then you'll be the one doing the giving and you might be free of this hero-worship stuff, because you'll be the heroine, the benefactor.

The idea she'd been toying with solidified. That was it. Flip their positions and she would lose that warm, heartbreaking gratitude tinged with desire that she always felt for Patrick. She would be the warrior-giver; the strong, stolid one.

Nice thought, too, except...what could she possibly do that would benefit Patrick? What did he care about? What did he need most?

The answer wasn't long in coming. It was a decent idea, a sound way to end things and to free both of them, too.

By rights she should have been dancing around the kitchen. Happy that she had found a solution for her aching heart and lips.

As it was...well, life didn't offer too many perfect skies, and this solution wasn't a totally guaranteed winner.

But at least it was something to sink her teeth into and at least if she was thinking of some way to help Patrick she wouldn't be thinking of kissing him.

At least when she was awake. Dreaming at night didn't count, did it?

CHAPTER TEN

PATRICK was nearing Able House. This was the day Jared was moving in, and he wanted to be there to—

"To what?" he said out loud. To meet with the man who might be the one to make Darcy happy, the man she might fall in love with?

No, I want to make sure he isn't going to hurt her, he told himself. He couldn't really even claim that he was here to make sure that Jared was a good fit for Able House, since he already knew he was. The guy taught self-defense to the disabled, a tremendously important task since opportunistic thieves sometimes targeted them.

Jared was also, Patrick had been told, outgoing, energetic and engaging, perfect for Able House. Maybe perfect for Darcy, too.

The thought left him grumpy and distracted, so he was caught off guard when he heard a commotion just ahead of him.

"What are you doing?" That was Darcy, but she wasn't speaking to him. One of the two troublesome neighbors, the one who had apparently shot his sprinklers over the sidewalk to discourage Able House residents from rolling past his house, was facing her. The man, Cal Barrow, was on the sidewalk while two men were shoveling dirt, making a terraced area on either side of the walkway. Cal's purpose was obvious. When he'd been running the sprinklers that day, Karen, the woman who'd been passing by and had been dressed for her job at a downtown office, had been forced off the sidewalk onto the grass. But the terraces and rocks the two men had piled up would prevent that.

Right now, however, Cal's future plans weren't Patrick's concern. The man was leaning toward Darcy. "Keep working," Barrow told his men. "I need more dirt right around here." And he picked up a handful of dirt and threw it where he wanted it, but some of it fell on Darcy.

"Oops," he said. "My apologies." But his tone sounded anything but apologetic. Instead he seemed…smug and satisfied.

Patrick was still fifty yards away. "Barrow!" he yelled as he charged toward the man. "Back off. You go near her again and you'll be missing your head."

The man whirled toward Patrick. "Back off, yourself, Judson. This is my property."

Patrick crossed his arms and looked down at the shorter man. "You are such a boring, sadistic creep, Barrow, and you're also wrong. The sidewalk and the parkway are public property. Darcy has every right to be here," he said, moving closer to the man, crowding him.

"But those kinds of technicalities don't matter to jerks like you, do they? I wonder what does matter to you. Those shops you run? So what would your customers think about your bully status? I can get that information to them in a matter of hours."

"Judson," the man said with a sneer. "You social snobs who have roots going back two hundred years think you're better than the rest of us, but…look at this woman. She doesn't have a pedigree. I've checked out every single person who lives in your pet project. Most of them are human mutts, too, so don't use that high-horse tone with me."

A red rage formed in Patrick's brain when Cal called Darcy a mutt. He drew back his fist. The man was lower than dirt and he was going to pay.

"Don't. Patrick don't hit him. Do *not*, under any circumstances, do that." Darcy's voice was soft. She spoke in a low command, not a yell, but her words effectively stopped Patrick's forward movement.

He turned to her, and Cal Barrow faded from his view. "Darcy, I'm not letting anyone hurt you."

"Then don't hit him. You can't. If you do, you'll make the news. Able House will receive bad press. Right now, other than the dirt, he hasn't done anything he could be charged with. His insults are protected by the First Amendment."

Of course. All that police academy training. She would automatically assess whether or not a crime had been committed.

Cal laughed, an ugly sound. Patrick tensed as hot anger flowed through him, but he didn't hit the man. "Listen to the little lady," Barrow told Patrick. "I haven't done anything wrong."

Patrick's anger escalated. Violence had never been a part of Patrick's life, but right now he wanted to let this guy have it in the worst way. He felt his control shredding. "Stay away from her," he said again.

"Patrick," Darcy said, and once again he forced control on himself. He focused only on her. "I want you to know this," she continued. "If he had touched me, I could take care of myself. I'm trained as a police officer, and knowing that my chair might hamper my ability to control the situation in case of an attack, one of the first things I did was bone up on self-defense."

Doubts assailed Patrick, and now—with this instance—and with the knowledge that he would soon be leaving her alone, he had to know. Had to hear it again. Would she say something just to keep him from getting hauled off to jail, to protect him?

He was pretty sure she would, but—

"You're sure?" he asked.

"I could have him on the ground if I needed to."

"Did Jared teach you that?"

"No, I learned this skill before I met him."

He was staring straight into her dark, expressive eyes now. He was going to have to believe what he saw there.

Cal laughed again, but Patrick wasn't laughing. He turned to Cal. "I wouldn't push it with Darcy. If she says she could take you down, it's true."

"I'd like to see her try."

"Then you'll see it. No complaints if I win?" she asked.

"Hah, you can't win!"

"Swear that you're inviting this," she ordered. "That this is an agreement, not an assault on my part."

Barrow laughed. "Like you're really gonna hurt me. Yeah, try it."

"Your call." She rolled forward. "Just try to knock me out of my chair. Go ahead."

Okay, that was enough, Patrick thought. He believed in her, but he wasn't going to let her mix it up with this guy. Even if she won, she still might get knocked about some.

But maybe nothing was going to happen, anyway. Barrow was looking sheepish. "No."

"Yes. Try it. Do it." She motioned for Cal to "come on."

"Hell," Patrick said. He hadn't thought it would get this far. "Darcy…"

Without warning, several things happened in quick succession. Barrow swore, something about stupid females. He roared and made a quick feint her way.

Darcy yelled, "Back off!" Then she slammed the heel of her hand hard against his face, snapping his head back. When he reeled, she hit him in the groin with her other fist.

Patrick barely registered what had happened, it took place so fast. But Cal was down on the ground, in the dirt, groaning, rolling, swearing, holding himself, trying to call Darcy names and keep from retching at the same time. "I'll sue!" The words he choked out were barely recognizable as words.

"Too late. I have your agreement on video," she said, pulling her camera phone from where she had slipped it into a loose pocket. "You have to pay attention when you're angry, Mr. Barrow, and not let yourself be distracted. You might miss something…like a woman holding a camera phone like this." She demonstrated how she had held the phone low at her side so that it was barely visible, but obviously effective. "Yeah, the picture's a little crooked, and it might not stand up in court, but I doubt a jury would convict me. What's more, do you really want anyone to know that I knocked you down? That would be *sooo* bad for your tough guy reputation, wouldn't it?"

Cal's response was to simply glare at her.

"Can we go now, Patrick?" she asked with a tense smile.

Without another word, they moved away together. They were almost to the front door of Able House and well out of Cal Barrow's view when Patrick stopped. He dropped his head for a full three seconds and let the blackness and fear that had enveloped him when he'd seen Barrow come at her take over. He counted to ten. Then, slowly, he straightened and looked her right in the eye. "If you ever do something like that again—Darcy, my heart completely stopped. If it hadn't worked and he had hurt you—"

"If he had hurt me, then, you could have hit him and I

wouldn't have stopped you. Then, it would have been a case of you protecting me from actual harm, not from his nasty words. You wouldn't have gone to jail for that or had your reputation damaged."

They had resumed their slow, forward movement, but now at the entrance to the building, Patrick leaned against the bricks and looked up to the sky. "You were protecting my reputation?"

"Someone had to do it. Heavens, Patrick, you were going to slug the guy over a little dirt and a bit of name calling."

"Darcy." He slid to his knees and took her face between his big palms. "You amaze me. Constantly. It wasn't just a bit of name calling. His words were ugly."

Her smile was tremulous. "Oh. You." As if that meant anything at all. "I've been called worse than that."

Which totally slayed him. He couldn't bear to think of her being subjected to that kind of thing, having to swallow insults. But…how could he tell her that? That he wanted to, needed to protect her if that ever happened again. She valued her independence so much, and heck, she had just knocked Cal Barrow on his rear end. What's more, she had been totally right about Cal not wanting the world to know about his humiliation, but Patrick still didn't trust the guy. Cal knew how to make nice when it suited his purpose. He had no problems lying in order to win people over and make Darcy and Able House a target if he had a good enough reason. Now he had a real reason.

Concern washed over Patrick, and still framing her face, he brushed his thumbs over Darcy's soft skin. Her silky curls twined around his fingers.

She was so close. He was so worried about her. Patrick had one thought. He wanted to tumble her onto his lap, he needed to kiss her silly and hold her tight so that he could—finally—

convince himself that she was safe and secure. Once he had her up against his heart, no one could touch her. He was on the verge of putting his thoughts into action when the sound of a slamming car door halted him.

Patrick looked up. He rose to his feet. Jared was sliding from his car into his chair. Had to be Jared. Up until now, Patrick had only seen pictures of the man. They didn't do him justice. His hair was California sun gold, his skin tanned, his biceps were the biceps of a man who worked out long and hard and often.

The man rolled toward them, but Patrick's focus was on Darcy, not on the man he was meeting for the first time. She was smiling, holding out both hands. "You made it," she said.

Jared gave her a long-suffering look. "Of course, I made it here, Darcy. Why wouldn't I?"

"That car…" she said. Patrick gave the car another look. It was long and sleek and black and obviously expensive. "That's the kind of car that makes you a target and you know it as well as I do. If someone tries to take that car from you, they just might—"

"Darcy, no mothering," Jared said.

She winced a bit at the word, and Jared looked as if he'd hit a bird.

Patrick ground his teeth. "Darcy," he said, but she held up her hand.

"Hell, Darcy, I'm sorry," Jared continued, "I know better than to use that word with you, but your…your nurturing when you know I can take care of myself…"

"I know," she said. "You're right. It's your car, your choice."

"And if you were the one with the expensive car…" Jared continued.

"You're right again," she agreed. "I wouldn't let you caution me about driving it."

"You'd bust my teeth out if I even suggested you couldn't protect yourself or your vehicle." Jared swung his head toward Patrick. "He must be the man who makes all this possible," he said, gesturing toward the building.

Darcy rushed forward to make introductions.

Patrick shook his head. "I supplied the start-up money and a little more. Everyone here supplies the work."

Jared nodded. "Sorry about losing my temper there, but Darcy gets a little overprotective. That's hard to take when she won't let the pendulum swing the other way."

"Tell me about it," Patrick said.

"So, you've tried to protect her, too?" Jared asked.

"Hello," Darcy said. "I'm right here, you two. You don't have to talk as if I'm not in the vicinity when I'm a living, breathing person, and I can hear you perfectly."

Patrick gave her a sheepish grin. Jared didn't even look slightly ashamed.

"So…maybe we should go inside so Jared can get settled in," Darcy continued.

"Bossy," Jared added as he followed her in. "But very cute," he told Patrick. As Darcy moved ahead, Jared lagged behind a bit, so Patrick waited.

"Too bad she doesn't want a relationship, right?" Jared asked. "Oh, but I'm gonna keep trying. You can't blame a guy for that, can you?" His tone was teasing, but the fact that he had made such a statement at all…

Patrick wasn't sure if Jared was merely being overly friendly or if he was trying to find out if Patrick would be a vindictive landlord if he shared Jared's interest in Darcy. Either way, it didn't change the score for Patrick. Dating Jared or not, Darcy was still off-limits. And after that episode with Cal Barrow, Patrick was even more worried about her.

"I can't blame you, but I'm sure you already know that Darcy's her own woman who makes up her own mind," Patrick said. Even so, he was definitely going to have to take action and make sure she was protected from volatile, hostile and possibly vindictive people like Cal. But if he did that…knowing how much she wanted, no *needed* to be in charge, would she hate him? Her need went beyond a mere desire for independence. It was a desire to be seen as a person who had overcome all those bad things that had happened to her. Single-handedly. If he took that from her, she might hate him.

And he might have to live with that…thousands of miles from her. His departure for France was less than two weeks away.

Darcy was in the kitchen alone three days later when Patrick came in suddenly. The expression on his face was so strange, so unreadable, so not like Patrick that—

"What is it?" Darcy asked. "Is it one of the girls?" Already her heart was breaking for him. She rolled forward.

Quickly he shook his head. "They're fine."

"Then what?" She was afraid she didn't want to know. But she had to know.

"It's nothing," he said. "I'm going."

"I know. In less than two weeks."

"No. The day after tomorrow. Change of scheduling. I just found out." And without another word he dropped onto a nearby chair, pulled her onto his lap and dragged her up against his chest. She looped her arms around his neck as he kissed her.

Desire and sadness and panic filled Darcy's heart as she tasted him, as he consumed her. Hungrily she kissed him back.

"Why so soon?" she asked as they came up for air.

"There's a gathering of government officials and community groups taking place in Madrid. Our project is being hailed as a good way to promote tourism and philanthropy and they want to know more. My presence has been requested."

Darcy tried a tremulous smile. "Publicity for your cause? That's…wonderful. It's what you've wanted."

"Yes. It's what I want."

But still he held her. He kissed her throat. He stroked her skin, his thumb brushing her breast, making her ache.

"It's what I've *always* wanted," he said, and now his voice sounded vaguely angry.

"Patrick?"

"Darcy, look at me. I'm sorry I'm manhandling you like this. I didn't even ask your permission. Again," he said as he eased her back into her chair. "I hope you know that I would never ask you to do anything that made you uncomfortable."

"I could have made you stop if I wanted you to."

He rested his forehead against hers. "Yes. You could have, but still…I don't want you to believe—I'll try not to let it happen again," he repeated.

No. There wouldn't be a chance for anything to happen between them, even if she wanted it to, Darcy thought with tears clogging her throat. Because he would be gone.

Somehow she had to live with that. She had to get past it, to make his last day here special and happy. A celebration.

It was time to put her plan in action. The only problem with the plan was…she had no time to plan.

CHAPTER ELEVEN

PATRICK was going slowly insane. This was the day he had been anticipating for years, and now that it was here, all he could think about was Darcy.

He'd run out of time with her, and...tension suffused his soul. That tension wasn't personal, he told himself. No, because that would be crazy. He and Darcy were polar opposites. They wanted different things. He was finally getting his freedom, a chance to fly free and explore his wild side. That would bring him and his company lots of attention, but it wouldn't be good for someone like Darcy. She hated attention, and this kind—it would be worse than what she was used to. It would involve celebrity. People wouldn't just be curious about her chair. They would want to know everything about her. They would dig up the school story, the fiancé story, the miscarriage story.

He frowned at that. He could never subject Darcy to that. He didn't want to hurt her. He didn't want anyone else to hurt her, either, he thought, remembering Cal Barrow.

Darcy might have bested the guy this time, but what about the next time or the next Cal Barrow?

"I'll take care of that," he promised himself. Already a

plan was in motion. That plan didn't make him feel any better about leaving Darcy tomorrow, but it was the best he could do on such short notice.

But his departure was still hours away. And Darcy was somewhere in the house. He could at least talk to her one more time.

Patrick opened the door of his study and stepped into the hallway.

The scent of sage and thyme and something roasting drifted to him. He breathed in and followed the aromatic trail. Cinnamon, nutmeg, coffee. Oh, yes, coffee. He would know that particular blend that Darcy brewed blindfolded.

He turned the corner.

And there they were. His family. All of them, his sisters and his brothers-in-law, seated around the table in front of a sumptuous candlelit meal. A small table had been set up for Charlie and Davey far away from the threat of candles and burns. Someone had put out little plates decorated with farm animals for them, and Charlie was leading Davey in a game of "what sound does this animal make?"

A banner hung over the doorway. It read, Happy Adventures, Patrick! Another one in the other doorway said simply, We'll Miss You. On the wall a long ribbon had been strung with photos of him and the girls over the years.

A large lump formed in Patrick's throat. "Well," he said. "What's all this?"

"It's your going-away dinner, big brother," Amy said, her voice a bit thick and teary. Patrick went to her and gave her a big brotherly hug.

"It's not forever," he said.

"It feels like forever," Cara said. "You'll be gone for six months and when Lane leaves in two weeks…nothing will be the same."

"I'll miss you, too," he told his sisters. "Like mad. Now, who's idea was this? Lane?"

"No. Not me. Cara and Amy and I were too upset to think straight. We might have managed a meal at a restaurant, but—this was all Darcy. She dug out the photos, and she handled all the decorations and the food. She wanted us to have one last special night together."

Someone entered the room then, but Patrick had grown so used to Darcy that he could feel her presence. This wasn't her. Olivia stood in the doorway with a bowl of food in her hands.

"Darcy?" he asked.

"In the kitchen."

Of course. "Would you ask her to come here, please."

Olivia gave a nod, and in moments Darcy was in the doorway.

She was dressed in pale blue with a silver clip in her hair and a snowy-white apron around her pretty, slim form. He wanted to simply stare at her, but that would have called attention to her and made her uncomfortable. "Thank you," he said. "Come sit with us."

Darcy's eyes opened wide. She twisted at the ties on her apron. "Oh. No. Me? Here? No."

"Yes. You did this," he said, moving toward her.

She shrugged. "It's just a simple meal. You were rushed. I thought you'd probably say private goodbyes, but I wanted everyone here for your last day. And anyway, I'd been planning it before that so it wasn't much work. Mrs. D. helped me find the pictures last week. I got help with the banners, of course." She seemed to run out of steam then. He could tell that she was ready to turn and run back into her safe little kitchen.

"Darcy," he said.

"Please. Stay here with us this time." That was Lane.

"Yes. Please. We mean it," Amy said.

"Really," Cara agreed. "You—everything is so nice. And you know that we're all on the verge of tears. None of us would have had the presence of mind to do this nearly as well as you have. You even made a special place for the boys and I know—well, thank you. Please, don't go."

"Mommy?" Davey's wavering little voice broke in. Patrick's younger nephew looked around as if he had just noticed that Amy wasn't at his side. Tears hung on his lashes. He looked so terribly sad and tiny.

Patrick heard a gasp. He turned to see Darcy looking at Davey as though her heart might break. She moved forward toward Davey half an inch, such a small amount that no one else probably saw, but Patrick did. Then, her hand flew to her throat and she slid backward, again just a touch. He couldn't help wondering and worrying if she was thinking of her baby. Her child would have been younger than Davey, but not by much.

"Come here, sweetie," Amy said, holding out her arms as Davey ran to her and she gave him a kiss. Darcy's expression was unreadable.

"Darcy?" Lane was asking. "Please. We meant it. Join us. It would make the evening complete."

Everyone seemed to be waiting for a response, and Darcy hesitated for a second. Then she gave a small, swift nod. "Thank you. I just have to do a few things. We can't—there's food to be finished. We can't eat our fingers."

The mood lightened. Lewis laughed and slung an arm around Cara, who managed a smile. Amy looked more at ease and so did Lane.

"Davey, boy," Richard said. "Mommy's going to sit here, not far from you. You be good and go keep Charlie company and he'll keep you company, too."

Davey hesitated. He chewed on one fat little finger, but

finally nodded. "Char," he said, pointing to Charlie and wandering to the smaller table. The two little boys hugged and went back to their game.

Everyone laughed, and only Patrick saw that, though Darcy smiled, too, her expression was still tinged with sadness. She turned, moved off and was just entering the kitchen when the doorbell rang.

"Who could that be?" Lane wondered.

Darcy halted. "I invited Angelise," she said. "But I didn't think she was going to make it. I thought—you said she was an old friend."

For several seconds there was silence.

Patrick stared straight into Darcy's eyes, but she looked away and he couldn't read her expression. What was this about?

Then, Cara nodded. "Thank you for thinking of her."

Mrs. D. came in, escorting Angelise. Angelise greeted everyone. Then she turned to Patrick. "I hate you," she said in a teasing tone, which had everyone turning their heads to see Patrick's reaction. "You're going to go away and take all the fun with you."

She came and sat beside him, pressing close. Patrick greeted her, but what he really wanted to do was march into the kitchen and ask Darcy a few questions. He wanted her beside him at the table. Now.

"You know, I've been thinking. I might take a trip to France soon, too," Angelise said. Which evolved into a discussion about foreign travel. In the meantime, Olivia and Darcy moved in and out with food. Olivia carried in special treats for the boys, but Patrick knew that it was Darcy who had thought of them.

The conversation swirled around him. He tried to pay attention to what his sisters and Angelise were saying. What he was noticing most, though, was Darcy.

When she came through the door the next time, she was carrying a wand lighter. Olivia had a dish. "Darcy's extra special peach flambé," Olivia said as she lit the concoction.

The glow from the flaming dish was reflected in the eyes of those sitting closest and a chorus of satisfied "ahs" added to the ambiance. The scent from the warm dish and the rum was spectacular.

Patrick looked up to voice his appreciation to Darcy, but she wasn't looking his way. She had turned toward the table in the other room. Suddenly a small cry left her lips.

"Davey, no, honey!" she cried, quickly maneuvering toward the child, who, Patrick realized, had found the cigarette lighter inside Angelise's purse.

Patrick stood, throwing off his napkin and interrupting Angelise midsentence as he shouted and charged toward Davey.

But Darcy had lifted the lighter from the little boy's hand already. "No, sweetie, I'm sorry, but it will hurt you," she was saying, rolling backward from the frightened face of the child.

"Charlie, stop!" Patrick yelled, but it was too late. Charlie had been rushing to see what the commotion was all about and had come up behind Darcy just as she was trying to back off and give Davey some space. The wheelchair bumped him. Charlie fell, and Darcy's wheel caught the edge of his foot.

He screamed in the high-pitched way only a terrified child can scream.

The world turned to slow motion. Every adult at the table rose and moved toward the area where Darcy and the children and Patrick were gathered. Tears started streaming down Davey's frightened face. Charlie crawled over to his mother, his arms reaching up to be held as she cried out.

And Darcy—the look in her eyes was the saddest thing Patrick had ever seen. She had raised her hands to cover her face, but those eyes…those stricken eyes that condemned herself completely…

Patrick could already see that Charlie was okay. He was cuddled against his mother and still whimpering and snuffling loudly, but beginning to move on to the next smile the way kids do.

"Darcy…" Patrick said.

She shook her head, hard. She closed her eyes. She broke his heart as two tears trickled from beneath her lashes. "I hurt him," she said with such anguish. "I hurt a—a baby. It was all my fault. I hurt a baby."

And Patrick realized in that moment that Darcy's fear of children, her unwillingness to cut herself a break went much deeper than that day with the little girl and the staircase. She was punishing herself for the loss of her own baby. She blamed herself for the miscarriage.

"Don't," he said. He realized that everyone at the table was starting to look at the two of them. He didn't care, not for himself, but for Darcy—

"I'm sorry," he said. "I know I promised not to do this again, but…"

He reached down and plucked her from her chair, pulling her into his arms. She was air, she was light, she was in pain.

"I'll call all of you before I leave," he told his sisters, and he strode out of the room, not even knowing where he was going.

As if Darcy suddenly realized what was going on, she tensed. "You can't leave. It's your farewell dinner."

"Watch me," he said. "It was a beautiful dinner, by the way, but I have something else I need to do now." He dropped a kiss on the crown of her head.

She looked up at him. "Patrick, please, you have to go back." But the anguish was still in her eyes.

He slowly shook his head. He climbed the stairs. As if his feet knew what his mind didn't, he found himself in the doorway to his bedroom.

Patrick stopped. He shifted Darcy in his arms. "Look at me, Darcy. He'll be fine. Children are very resilient."

"Not always, Patrick. No, they're not, and—I didn't even see him. He's so small. If he had been just a few inches closer and the tire had rolled over him, he would have been…I would have hurt him so much more…I…Patrick…"

Another tear slipped from beneath her lashes, and Patrick swore. He toed open the door and carried her in, sitting down on the bed with her on his lap. Slowly he rocked with her, shushing her and kissing her temples.

"I don't want to leave you," he said.

She froze. "You have to. Angelise is here. Everyone is here."

He hadn't meant that. "I don't care about Angelise."

Darcy looked up at him, a solemn expression on her face. "All right, maybe I made a mistake about her but someone else will come along. Someone like her."

"Darcy…"

"I *want* you to have someone like her," she said. "You have to do it, Patrick. You're used to family. You're going to miss all of that now that Lane is leaving home, and it's going to be difficult for you. I don't want you to be in this big house all alone when you come back. Do you understand?"

He understood. She wanted him to marry someone else, because she wasn't available.

"We'll see," he told her.

"You should get back," she told him again. "Would you mind—could I stay here just for a while? I can't go back down there."

"I'll stay with you."

She started to shake her head. "No, you have to…"

That did it. He turned with her, depositing her on the bed and sliding both of them down so that he was leaning over her, braced on his elbows while she was beneath him. "I have to kiss you," he said, finishing her sentence. "I'll never get the chance again. All right?"

Her response was a whimper as she reached up and pulled him down to her.

He slid his hands into her hair, loosening that fine wheat-colored silk from its bonds and fanning it out around her. When his lips met hers, he tasted salt from her tears followed by sweetness that was just…woman, all Darcy.

Heat rushed over him as he claimed her and she claimed him right back.

His gut instinct was to tell her that he didn't want to hurt her, but he'd heard Cerise complaining that she hated it when men treated her like a china doll, so he didn't say the words. Instead he told her what he was feeling.

"I want all of you," he said.

"Yes, I want that, too. Touch me," she told him.

He kissed her lips, her eyelids, her chin. He sipped at her throat, found a spot behind her ear that made her breath catch which made his pulse pound. When he reached the neckline of her apron, he reached behind her to untie the sash, pulled it from her and released the buttons that ran down the front of her dress. When he was done, he parted the lapels and kissed his way down her body. He stroked his palms down her sides.

She gasped, and he stopped. "Darcy?"

"I'm sorry. It's just that the line where the break was tends to be very sensitive in people with spinal cord injuries. It's the line between feeling and, in my case, less feeling and it… when you touch me there…"

He touched her there. She arched against him. He stroked her again, put his lips on her there.

She tore at his shirt, so he removed it.

She tugged on the waistband of his pants, so he disposed of them. Somewhere along the way, he tossed aside her dress, but his attention was on her, not on the clothes, not on the actions, just on her, on the expressions on her face, the sighs that escaped her lips.

He was on fire for her. And then, he was touching her in the places he had already learned made her burn. Her throat, her breasts, that wonderful, sensitive line she'd mentioned.

"You can love me," she said. "I want you to."

Her words nearly drove him right over the edge, and he had to close his eyes and concentrate not to leave her behind. That wasn't going to happen. He would be patient. He would wait forever, hold off forever.

"Patrick, touch me again," she whispered. "Touch me more."

He groaned. "Oh, yes, I intend to do that, but we are *not* rushing this. If this is the only night we make love, we're going to make it last."

Patrick slid his hand down her torso.

She gasped and mimicked his movements. Heat ripped through him.

He stroked. She caressed. He kissed. She nuzzled.

Then slowly, carefully—so carefully that he could barely stand it—he entered her and they began again. In aching slow motion he loved her. And the fire began to build.

Darcy's fingertips on his flesh were driving him insane. He moved in her. She welcomed him against her satiny skin. Touches. Caresses. He was losing control, trying to hang on.

"Patrick? I'm—I'm—" Her voice was breathless, strained.

"Yes," was all he could manage to say.

He brought her close, kissing the side of her neck and sliding his fingers over the exquisitely sensitive line of skin he'd discovered earlier as he joined their bodies again.

She cried out and wrapped her arms around him as his world teetered on the edge of bliss. Then everything turned to heat and stars and sun, and he fell apart.

When he returned to earth, and his breathing returned to normal, Patrick was disoriented. He looked down and realized that he held Darcy firmly at his side. He'd never had that happen before, that total loss of self. Thank goodness he hadn't crushed her.

She was gazing up at him and she brushed his lips with her fingertips. "Thank you."

"I think that's my line."

That brought a blush to her pretty body and she looked away. "I want you to promise me that you'll have a good time. Don't worry that I'll be remembering this night like some sort of pathetic novice who doesn't know anything about reality."

Patrick frowned. "What's the reality?"

She rested her arms on him and leaned in close. "That I want you to find an Angelise substitute and go shushing down mountains with her. Don't make me worry about you, and..."

"And?"

"And I meant what I said. I'm going to be really angry if *you* worry about *me*."

"Then I won't," he lied, "because you're a successful businesswoman with lots of friends." Which was the truth.

"You're darn right." She smiled at him, and then a wistful look came over her face. He tilted her chin up and gently kissed her lips.

"What?"

"I meant what I said," she repeated. "Thank you. You didn't

make me feel awkward or self-conscious. You made me feel wonderful. You were my first."

Later, when he'd taken her home and he was alone staring into the darkness, Patrick thought about that statement. He knew she hadn't meant that he was her first lover ever. She had been pregnant once before. She'd meant that he'd been her first since the accident, but…something was bothering him.

She wanted him to find another Angelise and date, maybe marry, and—and he had been her first.

That meant he wouldn't be her last.

A sharp pain whipped through Patrick. "Hell," he said to himself. "Don't go there." But he did, and he forced himself to accept it, because he wanted her to be happy, and it was clear that she wouldn't find happiness with him.

Maybe she would find it with Jared, or with someone else. Surely there would be someone else. But *he* had been her first.

And that wasn't a damn bit of consolation to him. He missed her already.

CHAPTER TWELVE

Two weeks later, Darcy sat in the kitchen. She held a bowl on her lap, stirring the contents.

"Are you going to beat that to death that, or will we eventually do something food-related with it?" Olivia asked.

Darcy looked up at Olivia, then down at the bowl. She shifted it in her lap and kept stirring. "It's going to be a cake. This is for Lane's "week of goodbyes.""

"Oh, yeah, she's having different friends over every day. What cake is it tonight?"

Again Darcy looked down at the batter and tried to concentrate. "Chocolate. I think. Yes, it's brown. Chocolate."

The look in Olivia's eyes called her back to attention. "What?"

"You never just say chocolate. It's always chocolate surprise, or hot fudge delight or too-good-to-be-true caramel. You are in bad shape. We need to do something. Fast."

That got Darcy's attention. "I'm fine. What are you talking about, Liv?"

"I'm talking about Mr. Judson."

Immediately Darcy flashed hot, then cold, then hot again. An ache so deep she could barely stand it took hold and she wanted to moan. Patrick was gone. He had kissed her and loved her, and it had been wonderful beyond anything she could have imagined, but now he was gone.

"You need to call him."

"What?" Darcy froze in midstir.

"I said, call him."

"What for?"

"Because you love him, you idiot. And you miss him."

"I do not!" But she did. Not that that could matter. He needed to be free, to fly, and she wasn't built for flying. More than that, though, was the other. He'd spent his life helping women, and just when he'd been on the verge of being free of that duty, she'd come along and he'd had to leap in and help her. Well, enough of that. She refused to be another duty holding him back.

And when he finally settled down, she wanted it to be with the right kind of woman: socially elite, accomplished, poised, beautiful and fully capable of giving him and caring for a houseful of precious babies.

"Not calling," she told Olivia stubbornly. "I've got things to do."

Olivia walked over and took the bowl out of her hands. "Now you don't."

"Hey!"

"I know how to make a cake," Olivia said. "You, pick up the phone."

"And say what?"

"That you love him."

"No."

"That you miss him, then."

Darcy thought about that. "No, he would worry."

"Then at least ask him who those people are that have been hanging around you lately."

"I know who they are. They're bodyguards. He's trying to protect me and the others at Able House from the Cal Barrows of the world."

"Well, then, you could at least thank the man. I'll bet you haven't even done that yet. Some appreciative woman you are."

Darcy opened her mouth. "I can't, Liv."

"He would call you if the tables were turned. Mr. Judson always treated everyone the same. He was always fair and polite and courteous to the lowliest of his employees."

"That's so not fair of you to remind me of that."

"Yeah, but it's true. Go in the other room. I won't listen."

It wouldn't matter. Darcy intended to make this very polite and extremely short.

But in the end, her plans went awry. The person who answered the phone was a woman who said that Patrick was unavailable. She was going to give him a massage, as soon as he woke up.

Patrick lay facedown on a table in the room adjoining the team locker room. He was exhausted. He'd fallen asleep waiting for Tanya, the team masseuse to finish with another competitor, and his unintentional nap had forced Tanya to wait for him to wake up. Now, Tanya was going to try to beat life back into his body, but his heart wasn't in the process. Because his body wasn't really the reason he felt so rotten.

"Your cell phone rang while you were out. I carried it into the other room and answered it so you wouldn't wake up. You need rest," she said, handing him the phone.

He needed a lot more than that, but Patrick was trying not to think about why he felt so miserable, especially since there was no solution to the problem.

Now, as Tanya began to pummel his muscles, he looked at

the record of received calls on his cell phone. The one that Tanya had told him about had come straight from his house.

His heart leaped just before reality set in. Probably Lane. Like Cara and Amy, Lane had called him several times already. He missed them, too, but he especially missed—

"Dammit," he said.

Tanya slapped him on the shoulder with her meaty hand. "Do not swear in my presence. I cannot unkink your muscles if you don't lie still and cooperate."

"That's okay. I'll keep the kinked muscles. Right now, I have to call my sister. Thank you for the massage."

"I barely began."

"I know. Bill me for the full session."

"You're going to be sorry, Mr. Judson. Your body has taken a beating these past two weeks. You look, if you don't mind my saying so, like heck."

"Like hell. I look like hell."

"Exactly." Tanya left.

Once she had gone, Patrick sat up and hung his head. He ran his fingers through his hair at the temple. He felt worse than he looked. No question why. He was in love with Darcy, who had made love with him, but had told him to marry someone else. Because she wasn't available.

"So, do it," he told himself.

Maybe he would. Maybe tomorrow. Right now he had to return Lane's call. He hoped that Darcy wasn't around. If she was, he just might do something stupid…like saying how he really felt about her, and that would make her feel guilty and unhappy. "No, I'm not doing that," he said to the empty room.

Darcy was wrestling with the centerpiece she was creating and trying not to envision what Patrick might be doing when Lane and Cara and Amy came into the room. Amy put Davey down and he gave everyone a big smile, then ran over to where Charlie was pulling things out of his toy bag.

"Charlie," Davey said. "Me, too."

Charlie gave his cousin a sigh and handed Davey a truck.

Instantly, Darcy went on full alert. For several reasons. The three sisters had never shown up in her kitchen all at the same time, they'd never looked at her in that strange way they were looking at her now, and…this was the first time Darcy had seen Charlie since the day she had run over his foot. What if he was afraid of her now? The thought of scaring a child…

"That looks great, Darcy," Amy said, indicating the arrangement of red and white candles, crystal glasses of cinnamon red candies and white mints and the cardinal and white University of Wisconsin-Madison logo. A small photo of Lane wearing her new red and white jacket was front and center.

"Love it," Lane agreed. "But I was wondering…"

"We were all wondering," Cara said, plopping down in a chair. "Have you heard from our brother lately?"

Darcy's panic antennae switched to full power. She felt as if she'd been hit by a sister sledgehammer. Not wanting them to see her face, she turned away and started rolling toward the other side of the room, trying to pretend she was intent on a task. "Not at all. Why do you ask?"

A small giggle sounded to her left and she saw that Davey was trying to play peekaboo with her from behind a chair whose rungs in no way hid his face. Against her will, she smiled, but the tension still gripped her as she heard Amy's next comment.

"He just called Lane, and…I spoke to him two days ago via video phone. He doesn't look well at all."

Darcy's heart stopped. Trying to hold on to her composure, hide her concern and not disappoint a child all at the same time, she cupped her palms over her face, then separated her fingers and peered out at Davey. "What do you mean, he doesn't look well?" she asked just as Davey giggled again.

"He looks positively ill." Lane's voice was choked, and Darcy turned slowly to face her.

When Davey came over and approached her, Darcy didn't even stop to think. She reached out and plucked up two plastic ladles and two plastic bowls and handed them to him.

"Two bows," he said.

"Two bows, indeed," she agreed, but her hands clenched. And not because she was speaking to a child.

"Patrick's sick?" Her voice came out too thin, slightly high-pitched.

"We don't know," Cara said. "That's the problem. He isn't saying. He isn't saying anything of substance."

Darcy fought not to let her feelings show. Panic. Fear. Love. More fear. She needed to see Patrick, to talk to him, but...

"I've tried to pry info from him," Amy said, "but he insists that everything is perfect. We're not sure if he's keeping things from us because he's still playing the guardian-brother who wants to protect his younger sisters from bad news or—we're beginning to think that maybe we're just too close to him to be objective. This is the first time Patrick has gone away for any length of time, and maybe we're just letting the fact that we miss him get in the way. We could be reading him wrong or just somehow selfishly hoping everything isn't perfect so that he'll come home sooner. We need someone more rational and sane than us to offer some perspective."

Oh man, were they really talking about her?

"You seem to have gotten to know him pretty well in the

weeks before he left. We just…I'm going to call him," Lane explained. "You talk to him and tell us what you think."

"No!" Darcy said, but as she said it she glanced to the side to see that Charlie had sidled up to her. He was holding out his hands and looking at her with big solemn eyes that quickly filled with tears. His lip was trembling in that way that little children's lips trembled, the way that made your heart break.

"Oh, Charlie, I wasn't yelling at you, sweetheart," she said. "Did you want some dishes, too?"

He nodded and she wasn't sure which one of them was going to cry first. "Here," she said, rolling back a bit and digging into a drawer. "Here's a whole set of measuring cups and spoons. Okay?"

Charlie nodded and ducked his head. He took his toys and retreated to a corner while Darcy's throat closed up. For so many reasons.

She looked up to see the sisters staring at her. "Will you do it?" Lane asked. "I'll get a video line going."

Would she do it? Yes. Her heart filled with tears and fear. Patrick was ill. She loved him and she was going to kill him if he wasn't taking care of himself.

"Yes, please call Patrick," she said, and she prayed that his sisters didn't know just how much this meant to her.

Patrick's nerves were strung tight. This was the second time in an hour he'd spoken to his sisters. Something was up. Lane had put the call through, but now she was being evasive, claiming that the other girls wanted to speak with him, but he had spoken to Cara and Amy only yesterday.

"Hey, big brother, how's it going?" Cara asked.

"Yeah, how's it going, Patrick? What did you do today?" Amy asked.

"I'm fine. I was paramotoring." But then she already knew that. He'd told her that yesterday. And…Lane had set up in the kitchen. It was the first time she'd placed a call there.

His head began to pound. The camera didn't take in all of the room. He studied the perimeters of the viewing area and frowned. Where was Darcy? He tried not to think about the fact that she might be with Jared…or someone else. Maybe she was dancing. Or maybe Eleanor had sent her off on a catering job or maybe she was wheeling down the sidewalk from his home to hers. She'd have to pass Cal's.

Patrick scowled.

"What?" Lane asked. "What's wrong?"

"Nothing."

"Good. That's good. I—Darcy's here."

Now his heart began to thunder. He cursed the limits of the video linkup. Where was she?

She came into view, moving closer to the camera. "Patrick." That was it, just that soft sound, like a caress. "Your sisters were right. You're not taking care of yourself."

"I am." A total lie.

Now that cute, stern look he loved came over her face. "I'm not your sisters. I'm not going to treat you with kid gloves or lie to you. You look like you've been staying up all night and day and not eating right."

He held his hand up. "I'm fine, just brilliant. But you…are you getting out of the kitchen?"

She smiled and his whole body ached. "I'm a cook. I'm supposed to be in the kitchen."

"But not all the time. And those neighbors…have they given you any more trouble?"

"Nothing I can't handle."

"Dammit, Darcy. You look as if you've lost weight."

She blinked and looked slightly evasive. "Didn't anyone ever tell you not to ask about a girl's weight? That's not like you, Patrick. You've usually got that etiquette thing down pat."

Ah, she was teasing him. He loved it when she teased him, but not when he couldn't be there with her or touch her. This damn video connection wasn't nearly three dimensional enough. You'd think that a man with his money could convince someone to invent a device that captured the essence of Darcy.

"You're right. No weight questions. Are you…enjoying life, then?"

She nodded. That was it? Just a nod? No details?

"And…" He frowned. "Everything is all right at Able House, isn't it? I get reports but they don't really tell me the half of it."

"We're okay," she said quietly. "You shouldn't worry."

All right, there was a loaded sentence. "I could have postponed this trip, done more before I left," he said, hating the feeling that he wasn't there to control things.

"Patrick, look at me," Darcy said. So quietly. Her voice was almost a whisper, but it mesmerized him.

He looked at her, he connected with her. "*Don't* worry," she said.

"You know I'm going to."

She frowned. "Are you…what are *you* doing?"

He rattled off a list of activities he'd taken part in during the past two weeks in various stops in Italy, Spain and France. Skydiving, bungee jumping, white water rafting in Chamonix. But he didn't want to talk about himself. "Have you and Jared gone dancing anymore?" Did that sound jealous? "And Cerise," he added, just in case he had sounded jealous.

"Once." Her answer told him nothing. "Are there…are there a lot of parties?"

"I suppose there are quite a few. The company arranges events during the day and entertainment for the evening."

As he spoke, he saw Charlie appear at Darcy's side. Where were his sisters? Why weren't they taking care of Charlie? Didn't they know how difficult this was for Darcy? No, of course they didn't. He had never told them about her past, and Darcy wouldn't have told them, either.

"Is Cara there?" he asked suddenly.

Darcy blinked and slid back. Cara moved into her spot, but he didn't want to discuss this in front of everyone, not even his other sisters. Charlie was Cara's and it should only be her. "I have something to ask you, but…take the call in the other room, all right?"

Cara's expression turned to alarm, but she clicked off the monitor. When her voice resumed, they were audio only. "Patrick, what is it? What's this about?"

"Darcy. It's all about Darcy." In as brief a manner as he could, he explained that she needed to be careful with Charlie and Darcy.

"Charlie is the best," he told her. "I love him to pieces, but Darcy is fragile. Especially after that dinner, she'll be…don't make her take care of him."

"I didn't know, Patrick. I didn't ask her to take care of him and now that I know, I wouldn't. I—"

"I'm not blaming you, Cara, but I just…" He rubbed the back of his neck. "I don't think I did well by Darcy. I want her to be happy, and it's driving me nuts that I don't have the power to make sure that she is."

Cara hesitated. "Is that why you look so beat-up? You're worrying, the way you used to worry about us when we were growing up."

No, it wasn't like that at all.

"Something like that," he said.

"We'll look out for her," she told him. Cara was, he knew, a woman of her word. Her promise should make him feel better, so why didn't it?

Because he wanted to be the one. Even as the thought formed, Patrick realized that there was more than one meaning for that statement. He wanted to be *the one*.

But that wasn't a choice that was open to him.

"I'll want a full report next week, sweetheart. On all of you."

And if things weren't all that they should be, he was going to do something drastic.

CHAPTER THIRTEEN

DARCY looked up when Cara came into the room and found the other woman studying her intently.

"What?" Darcy asked.

Cara shook her head. "So, what's the verdict on Patrick?"

"He looks…tired."

"Worse than tired," Lane said.

"He doesn't look like Patrick. It's as if something's missing from him," Amy said.

"It's as if someone turned off the light inside him. His essence, the thing that makes him Patrick has been dimmed." The second that Darcy uttered the words, the girls turned toward her.

"Yes," they all agreed.

"He's worried about you," Darcy offered.

But the sisters exchanged a look. "He asked an awful lot of questions about *you*," Amy said.

"He knows that I have Lewis and Amy has Richard and Lane has school, but it's Darcy he's worried about," Cara agreed.

Darcy's heart hurt. "That's so unfair."

The sisters looked startled and Darcy shook her head. "I don't mean that what you're saying was unfair to me. I meant that it's unfair that Patrick should be worrying. He's done all he could for me. He's even hired bodyguards to watch over us at Able House."

"Yes, but that wouldn't be enough for him. Patrick's very hands-on. Not being able to prevent our parents' deaths ate at him. I think that colored his life, so when one of us got hurt and he couldn't keep it from happening or cure us, he walked the floor and pestered the doctors even though he knew they were doing their best. He did the job of two parents, so no, hiring a bodyguard wouldn't dispel Patrick's concerns."

Cara shook her head. "It's you. You're the one."

Darcy bit her lip. Her throat felt tight. "He's supposed to be playing, not worrying about me. I told him I wanted him to find a wife. That and all those fun things he wants to do should be all he's thinking about."

Lane raised one brow in a gesture that was so like Patrick's that Darcy had to swallow hard to keep from remembering. "A wife? I wish, but despite all our attempts…apparently not likely yet. I've heard from friends over there that there are plenty of women falling over him, but when he attends functions, he goes alone and leaves alone."

Darcy tried not to react to that. Relief and distress warred within her.

"Look. Darcy," Cara said. "Patrick is obviously worried sick about you. How can he enjoy himself when he's so concerned?"

"I don't think he's sleeping right, either," Darcy said. "He really will get sick if he doesn't take better care of himself. I'll call him back and reassure him. I'll tell him I'm just great."

"You already did. We did, too. Numerous times. He's asked about you every time any of us has spoken to him. I don't know exactly what's going on between my brother and you, and maybe it's none of my business. Or it wouldn't ordinarily be my business, but if neurosing about your well-being is affecting his health and well-being—well, whatever your relationship is, it's…"

"It's my fault," Darcy said. "From the beginning he knew I had issues." She launched into a brief explanation of her past. When she got to the part about children, Cara nodded sadly.

"That's why he was so worried just now that I was letting Charlie crawl all over you."

Darcy bit her lip, thinking about how she had scared Charlie, but also about how he had been so quick to forgive her. What a charmer he was and…he was Patrick's nephew. Her heart swelled, thinking of the two little boys and their uncle. She took a deep breath and nodded. "Patrick knows where I'm vulnerable. I wish…I should have done more to show him that I can be strong. I hate the fact that I haven't made more of an effort to show him how much of a difference he made in my world. He brought me out of myself."

There the three of them went, exchanging those secretive looks again. Darcy wondered what it must be like having sisters so close to you that they could read your expressions.

"You could still do that," Amy said. "Show him that you're strong, I mean."

"Yes, Amy's right," Lane said. "I can guarantee that telling Patrick you're fine is never enough. It never was with any of us. He always needed to see proof."

Darcy blinked. She and Lane studied each other. "So, you think that if I show him that I'm moving on with my life and that I'm capable of going it alone without his assistance, then he'll be able to move on, too?" She frowned. "Do you really think that's why he looks so ill? Maybe it's something worse, something else."

"I don't know. Patrick drives himself. He demands more

of himself than any man I know. It's as if he thinks he should be able to work miracles. Remember when Lane was in the hospital with a concussion and we didn't know if she was going to come out of it?" Cara asked.

Amy nodded. "Patrick looked just like that, then. As if he had aged ten years in a day. I came across him when he thought he was alone and the devastated expression on his face scared me to death. Darcy, I—Cara and Lane and I—Patrick's more like our father than our brother, but we can't do anything for him. You're the key. You have to be the one to help him."

Darcy wanted to do that. She needed to be with Patrick and see for herself that he was safe and strong and happy. "But, he's in France," she whispered. "And I'm here."

Cara didn't hesitate. "That's the one thing the three of us can do. We can get you there and we can get you in, but you have to do the rest."

"You have to have a plan," Amy added. "If you go over there and whatever happens increases Patrick's anxiety about you…"

"Maybe we should just ask him to come home and see how she's doing for himself," Lane suggested.

"No," Darcy said. "This is his trip of a lifetime. He's put heart and soul into this. And it's important. Think of all those children his charities are going to help. I'm not asking him to cut his trip short or take time away just to come check me out."

"So…you're going over there then?" Amy asked.

For ten seconds Darcy allowed panic to overtake her. To get on a plane and travel around the world chasing a man she was in love with in order to convince him that she *wasn't* in love with him and that she had conquered all her fears when she hadn't done anything of the sort was taking a major chance. Not only with her own heart but with Patrick's health and well-being. Because if she messed this up and came across as needy in any way, he was going to blame himself for her vulnerability. Everything she knew about him and everything his sisters had told her pointed to that.

She took a deep breath. "Anything I do or say has to be realistic and utterly convincing. Patrick has a way of seeing through me."

"Can you act?"

"No."

Lane opened her eyes in alarm.

"I can't act well enough," Darcy clarified. "I'm not good at playing a part, so if I'm going to show Patrick that I've moved on and made a new life for myself, it has to be real. I have to believe it, too. So...if you'll give me two weeks and set up the travel arrangements, I'll just head home and...quietly try to reinvent myself."

"Who will you be when this is done?" Olivia asked, entering the kitchen.

"I haven't a clue," Darcy said, trying to keep the despair and concern from her voice. She just hoped that the woman who would emerge from the cocoon in France would not be in love with Patrick.

She wanted to set him free. It would be so much easier to do that if she didn't care about him so much.

Patrick paced the floor of his hotel room. He was supposed to be getting ready for a meeting and then attend a dinner, but he had just received an e-mail from Lane telling him that Darcy would be arriving within the hour for some sort of event she had been asked to cater. What was that about? And why hadn't Darcy contacted him herself?

A part of him didn't care. He just wanted to see her and hear her and touch her.

"You're not touching her, buddy," he told himself.

But he damn well was going to ask her a lot of questions. He whipped out his phone and called the number Lane had included in the message.

Two rings. Three rings. Four. Darn it, the voicemail was going to kick in. He didn't want to leave a message. He wanted to hear her voice and he wanted...*intended* to meet her at the airport. What airline was she flying? Lane hadn't said. He was on the verge of calling Lane when the telephone in the room rang. He picked it up.

"Patrick?" Darcy's voice slipped right through his body, soft and sexy and—

"Where are you?"

"In the lobby. May I come up?"

Yes, yes, yes. Hurry. But she would need to find someone to help her with her bags and direct her to his room and—

"Stay there."

He barely waited for her assent before he sprinted out the door and down the hall, ignoring the elevator for the much faster stairs. Emerging from the stairwell, he bolted into the lobby and saw her.

His heart turned three somersaults. She had done her hair differently and the soft tendrils brushed her cheeks, accenting those phenomenally expressive eyes. She was holding out her hands to him and a gorgeous smile lifted her lips and lit up her eyes.

"Patrick, I'm so happy to see you," she said. He had never seen her more lovely. A glow seemed to emanate from her. She looked healthy and happy.

He walked straight toward her, took her hands and bent to kiss her cheek. That wonderful woman and lemon scent he remembered filled his senses and nearly brought him to his knees. He wanted to inhale her. "Are you staying here?"

"Um, on the fourth floor. Amy made the arrangements." Then, she frowned slightly. "That is, I would have made them myself, but I had so many things to do before I left that I just…let her."

"My sister made hotel arrangements for you?"

"Yes, and the flight arrangements, too. Your sisters are pretty efficient, Patrick. Someone must have trained them well. I wonder who." She wrinkled her nose and laughed. Patrick wanted to groan. She was the most incredibly, sexy, exciting woman he'd ever met. How could he have forgotten that?

"I see you're just as sassy as ever."

"That's a good thing, right?" she asked. For just a second, he thought he saw her hesitate. Then she rushed on. "You're probably wondering why I'm here."

"Lane said something about an event you were catering. International stuff, Darcy?"

She shrugged. "I know. Isn't it crazy and great? I was talking to Eleanor one day and she told me about some friends she had who liked to throw parties, and the next thing I knew they were offering me a job! A brunch for a big gathering of friends and family they were having. How could I turn that down? It's not like I get invited to France every day."

A bellman arrived at that moment. "Mademoiselle Parrish?"

Patrick looked at Darcy. "What's your room number?" he asked, preparing to give the man directions and a tip.

But Darcy was already talking to the man. "Guillaume, is it?" she asked in somewhat halting French, tilting her head up to see the man's name tag in a way that emphasized her lovely neck. "How do you do, Guillaume? It's my first time to France, I'm afraid, so I apologize in advance for speaking French so poorly." At least that was the gist of what she said. There were also a few extra words in there that made no sense whatsoever.

Patrick cleared his throat, planning to help out. He spoke perfect French, and Guillaume knew it. They'd had numerous conversations in the hallway this past week.

But Guillaume was clearly charmed. He gave Darcy an intimate smile. "I speak *un peu*, I mean, a little Anglais," he said, his accent almost as bad as Darcy's command of French. "You—tell me whatever you need. I'll help you. Anything."

Darcy looked at the man with a teasing twinkle in her eye. "Guillaume, you're not giving me special treatment because of my chair, are you?" she asked, motioning toward her wheels.

"Maybe just a very little," the man said, "but mostly because you are polite about the language, you have a nice smile and because you're a very beautiful woman. I like you."

Her soft laughter rang out, and Patrick wanted to lean closer. He wanted to push Guillaume aside. "I think I like you, too, Guillaume," she said as she gave him her room number and he headed off with her bags.

She clearly liked Guillaume. She had practically been flirting with the handsome Frenchman. Okay, Patrick thought, for a man who wasn't prone to violence, he definitely wanted to *hit* the man now. No, that was wrong, and it wasn't fair, except…he'd seen Guillaume flirting with the maids. He was pretty sure he was dating several of them. He had an urge to tell Darcy to be careful with men like that, but that wasn't right, either. Darcy was an intelligent woman with a good head on her shoulders and she had spoken to Guillaume, a total stranger, in a completely uninhibited way that was unusual for her. She had even called the man's attention to her wheelchair. What was going on here?

Patrick looked down. Apparently what was going on was that Darcy was looking at him as if wondering what the holdup was.

"You probably want to go to your room and rest," he said, wishing he had more time with her but not wanting to exhaust her.

"Are you kidding me, Patrick? I'm in France, it's late and tomorrow I have to get up at the break of dawn and get ready to prepare a brunch. Right now I want to…I want to do lots of things."

He grinned. "Lots of things?"

She blushed. "Yes."

"Like what?"

"I—I well I guess I don't have a clue. What do people do in France?"

Patrick laughed. The excitement on her face delighted him. She was playing with the wheels on her chair and he could see that she was ready to be off. "They live. They shop, work, go to museums, they eat. You are going to love that about Paris. The food is…"

"An orgasmic experience?" she asked with a wicked smile, and he remembered the first day that they had met.

"Well, nothing surpasses your chocolate mousse, but you'll love it."

"That's it. Take me on a tour of restaurants!"

"A tour?"

"I don't have much time."

Ah. The emptiness that had disappeared completely when he had heard she was coming returned. "How much?" His voice was a bit too clipped. Had she noticed? Would she guess how much it mean to see her?

"Two days. Not quite that. More like forty hours before I have to head back to the airport. I have to get back to—to help with some—an event." Darcy got that old nervous look in her eyes, she licked her lips, but then she shook her head as if to get rid of something that was bothering her. She smiled again.

"Another event? You're a busy woman."

"You have no idea. I don't have a moment to myself. Busy all the time, night and day."

"Your nights, too, Darcy?" What did she mean by that?

She blushed, which only intrigued him more. "Oh, you know, dancing, partying, stuff."

"Partying?" he said. But it was the word "stuff" that caught his attention. Did she mean men? Unbidden the memory of Darcy in his arms, her delicate skin beneath his questing lips invaded his thoughts.

Patrick took a deep breath. He didn't have the right to ask her about men. She was free to date whom she pleased, and…darn it, she was only here for two days. For tonight anyway, she was his.

"I'll walk you to your room and you can get changed. Then we'll go have a movable feast."

She nodded, but neither of them moved. Her gaze locked with his. And somehow his feet took him closer to her. He took her hands and kissed the palms. "I've missed you, Darcy Parrish. No one else plays it as straight with me as you do."

For half a second he thought he saw something dark and sad in her eyes. Had he pushed her too far? Had he let his feelings show too much?

"I'll find my room," she said. "And I'll meet you back here in twenty minutes."

Darcy broke into a cold sweat on the way to her room. What was she doing? How had she ever thought she could handle this?

The girls had given her a crash course in French. She'd done all kinds of crazy things to throw this together fast. The whole situation was surreal. The energy involved in making this happen had kept her from panicking.

But, when she had seen Patrick, her heart had flipped over completely and when he'd touched her—she stopped right in the middle of the hallway and sat there, her hands crossed over her chest as she counted to ten and fought for composure.

Thank goodness she had insisted that this trip be kept short. She couldn't keep up this charade with Patrick for long. Smiling and pretending that all she felt for him was friendship when…well, what else could she do? While they had been talking several gorgeous women had entered the lobby and looked as if they intended to approach him. They had looked as if they knew him, as if they wanted to know him very intimately, or maybe already did. But they obviously wanted the chance to get him alone because none of them had actually come close enough to speak to Patrick. And now…

"Get hold of yourself, Darcy," she muttered. "You can do this. You can see that he's feeling more at ease already. And when this is over, there's only one more thing you have to do and then he's free and clear. You'll have done one good thing for him and ended it right. Don't blow it."

No, she refused to mess this up. If she appeared in any way lost or in love or needy—it would hurt Patrick so much to have to let her down easy.

"Never going to happen." She took a deep breath, plastered on that air of confidence she'd been practicing, changed into something attractive but not provocative and went down to meet Patrick. This was going to be so hard…and so wonderful.

CHAPTER FOURTEEN

THE evening passed more quickly than Darcy would have liked. She was incredibly tired now that jet lag was setting in, and she had to get up early to prepare for the brunch, the job that she had all but begged Eleanor to help her secure. The people who were hosting the brunch hadn't even been planning anything at all until Eleanor called them up and raved about how she knew this simply marvelous chef who would be passing through Paris for a couple of days and would like to try her hand with some of the local produce, wines and cheeses. Now, Darcy had to live up to the billing.

But tonight there was Patrick, if she could just keep her eyes open and her mind on the task at hand and off the fact that she wanted to kiss him in the worst way.

"There?" she asked. "I'm not so sure." They were headed for their last restaurant of the evening. He had chosen ones that were known for fine dining, and she had done her best to come out of her shell, to be witty and open with the staff and even with total strangers who were simply dining there as well. In short, she had acted totally unDarcylike. Because that was what Patrick needed to see, that she was making progress and healing. That he had no reason whatsoever to worry about her.

"You don't want to go there?" he asked. "I haven't been there yet, but it's gotten great reviews."

Maybe, but at the moment the crowds had thinned. There was a sterility to the chrome and glass. And the tables were big. She would be many feet away from Patrick. And tonight…oh, just tonight she wanted one more chance to be close to him.

"That one," she said, pointing to a small, intimate looking place on the corner across the street.

"You're sure?"

She laughed. "It's kind of plain, isn't it? I'll bet you never eat in ordinary little places like that."

Looking up, she saw that Patrick was looking a little sheepish, but he was smiling, too. "You don't do you?" she asked again.

"I do tonight. I have it on excellent advice that it's a place I should try. My favorite chef tells me so."

"What if it's awful? You'll never trust me again."

"I trust you implicitly. You're always honest with me, and you'll admit if you've made a mistake."

Honest? She wasn't being honest with him now. At best she was leaving lots of things out. But she was never going to tell him that she had come over here to do a snow job on him.

She sighed. Oops. Major error, that sigh. "Sorry, I'm a little jet lagged," she said.

"You should be in bed."

"No!" She didn't want to give up this time.

"Alone," he clarified. "I wasn't implying that you should be in *my* bed."

"I would like to be in your bed." Okay, all this playacting and being totally open and outgoing was having a bad effect on her. "Forget I said that."

"Not in this lifetime."

"It was the lack of sleep talking. I probably couldn't do much, anyway."

"I could do all the heavy lifting."

Excitement rose within her. But oh, why had she even started this conversation? She couldn't survive making love with Patrick and leaving again. Look at what one night in his arms had done to her. She was pathetic and needy, all the things she had fought not to be for years.

"Let's go in," she said, but then she realized something.

So did he. "Those are very narrow aisles." No room for her chair.

Embarrassment flooded her face. These were the kinds of things that made her feel as if she didn't belong. If she sat here long enough someone would notice and realize the reason they were milling about outside. That was when the pitying looks or the averted faces would begin.

And she knew that Patrick realized her distress just as sure as she knew that darkness fell every night. Once that registered with him, the man was going to go into all-out, full protective mode. He would be worried about her; he'd try to save her. That was the very thing she had come over her to put a stop to.

"Pick me up, please," she said.

"Darcy?"

"Well, it's totally clear that I'm not going to roll or walk in there, isn't it? And I'll bet you're almost strong enough to carry me." She said this rather loudly as a couple was passing. When they looked at her, she smiled and waved as Patrick was lifting her into his arms, holding her against his heart.

"Do they have good desserts here?" she called out in her very bad French.

"Oui, mille feuille," the woman said.

"Ah, *merci*," Darcy said with a big smile. She waited until the couple had gone. "What did she say?" she asked.

Patrick laughed and pulled her closer. "She implied that they had good Napoleons here," he whispered near her temple.

Darcy fought to keep breathing. "I love Napoleons. Let's go inside." Oh, she needed to get inside. She needed Patrick to put her down. If he didn't do it soon she would grab him and press her aching lips to his.

But the little shop was closed when they tried the door. The man was just locking the door. *"Demain,"* he told them. "Tomorrow."

Which only served to remind Darcy that there wouldn't be a tomorrow with Patrick. She had already asked him what was on his schedule tomorrow and he had a ball he had to attend. The day after that she'd go back to Chicago.

By the time they got back to her room she was so weary that she could barely keep her eyes open. Patrick saw her to her door. "I'll see you bright and early tomorrow," he told her.

She blinked.

He smiled. "I'll bring the Napoleons. And coffee."

Then he kissed her on the forehead and left her.

Dratted man. Now she would never be able to sleep.

Patrick stood back and watched Darcy work the room. He had been with her since early morning and she was still going strong. She was simply amazing. And different. In a sassy, sexy way that he found incredibly tempting.

Was this the same woman who normally hid in the kitchen? Couldn't be, because she had been roaming the room for the past two hours, making sure dishes were replenished and that everyone got a taste of each dish. She even talked with apparent ease about the preparations and the history of some of the dishes. She supervised the staff she'd made arrangements for and stayed until the last dish was cleaned and put back on the rental truck.

Then she said an affectionate goodbye to the hosts.

"You are adorable," the woman said.

"And a fantastic cook," her husband agreed.

"And a good judge of men," the woman went on. "Your husband is very handsome." Just as if Patrick wasn't there.

For the first time Darcy looked flustered. "We aren't married," she said.

"But he desires you. I see it in his eyes when he looks at you," the man said.

"And you look at him the same way," His wife added.

Total panic filled Darcy's eyes. "Desire isn't nearly enough," she said. And didn't that say everything he needed to know about how she felt about him?

He should just let her go about her business, and he should go on to his affair tonight. "Come with me tonight," he whispered as they neared the hotel.

She looked up at him with confusion. "I can't."

He gave a curt nod. "You have things to do."

"Not a thing, but…" She looked down at herself.

"Not a problem," he told her. "I have to warn you, though. There will be a lot of people there."

"Angelise?" she asked. "I—Cara called me today to check in, and she said that she'd heard Angelise was here."

Cara had called Darcy and not him? What was that about?

"Angelise gets around."

"She wants to marry you."

"We're friends."

"But there are other women here who wouldn't mind wearing your ring, either. I've seen them. They're like you."

What the hell did that mean? Was she talking about her wheelchair? Her social status? Patrick wasn't quite sure he cared. Darcy had told him that he should marry. She'd made it very clear over and over that she wasn't interested in marriage.

"I'll be dancing with you tonight," he said. It was a dare, a claim. He wanted her last night here to be spent with him.

"I'll take you up on that," she said.

"I can't wait." And that was no lie.

Focus, focus, focus, Darcy told herself. She had come here with a goal in mind, to demonstrate to Patrick that she was a woman on the move, a woman who had her life together and who no longer feared being the center of attention, so tonight she had to make her case. Cross any t's and dot any i's she hadn't managed to cross or dot yet.

But she also had another goal: to grasp this last chance to soak in as much of Patrick as she could. When she got home she had one more very important task. She had to make sure that everyone at Able House was committed to Patrick's plan for them. Then she was going to leave Able House and set out on her own. She couldn't stay connected to Patrick and have any chance of happiness.

Tonight really would be their final goodbye, at least in person, so Darcy rolled into the ballroom prepared to act her heart out and make as many memories as possible. That strange sensory trick that made her instantly aware of him helped her locate him almost immediately. He was surrounded by men, but there were also a number of beautiful, willowy mobile women with perfect hair and makeup and shoes crowding close to him. Lots of them sported bare shoulders, cleavage and dresses to die for whereas she was wearing a very simple and inexpensive red gown. No cleavage. Not that she had much in the way of cleavage.

Don't think that way, she told herself. Remember, you have to be the new Darcy for Patrick. Paste on a confident smile.

The magical thing was that the second he saw her and smiled at her, her smile became real, too. She looked up and down that tall, broad-shouldered form. She remembered how that dark hair had felt against her fingers, how those green eyes had gazed into hers as he caressed her, how that mouth had felt against her skin.

Nothing could have stopped her from entering that crowd then. For once Darcy was happy that her wheelchair attracted attention, because the sea of people parted to let her pass.

Patrick met her halfway. "Darcy, you look amazing."

"So do you. You look…hot," she said as the people closest to them laughed. Darcy blushed. "Sorry," she said to everyone. "I have a big mouth."

"Don't apologize. Who are you, beautiful lady? Judson, introduce us," some man said.

Patrick looked askance at her, and Darcy nodded.

"This is Darcy, a wonderful chef and a wonderful friend. If you ever need a caterer—"

"I'm your woman," Darcy said, dipping her head in a mock bow.

"Interesting," another man said.

"Where has Patrick been hiding someone as gorgeous as you?" another male voice called out.

"In his kitchen, but I'm a free agent now," Darcy said, remembering that conversation with Angelise.

"Well, then—"

"Time to go," Patrick said. "Didn't you promise me a dance, Darcy?"

She smiled up at him and was surprised to see that he was

frowning at her. She'd thought that conversation had gone pretty well. It took some deep breathing to put herself out there in such a public way, but no one had seemed to be offering pity. The banter had been light.

"I hope I didn't embarrass you with that comment about you being hot," she said, as she and Patrick left the crowd behind.

He shook his head. "I think you just made my reputation," he said with a chuckle. "Every guy who heard that is going to be envious. I walked away with the girl in the red dress with the wild, wicked mouth. Half those guys want to sleep with you now."

"What do the other half want to do?"

Patrick laughed. "They want to sleep with you, too."

"My, your friends certainly have one track minds. How do they get any business done?" she teased.

"I haven't a clue. They're total boneheads. Don't even look at them," he teased right back, and when she looked up into his eyes and saw him smiling at her, Darcy's heart felt as if it was expanding so much that her chest wouldn't be able to hold it.

"I wouldn't think of it," she said. I've missed you, she thought. "I don't have time to look at them. You and I are going to dance, aren't we?"

"Absolutely."

"You'll be okay with the wheelchair?"

"I can't believe you're even asking me that. By now you ought to know me better. I want to dance with you, and your wheelchair is how you get from place to place. If anything, you'll be the one having a problem with me. You know what you're doing, while I don't have a clue."

"Don't worry. I'll be gentle with you," she teased.

"Then there's no problem, is there?" he asked. "I'll trust

you to give me cues. I did watch a few wheelchair dance videos on the Web in anticipation of this moment."

"Then you do have a clue."

"Seeing isn't doing," he quipped. But in the end, Darcy decided that Patrick must have either watched those videos carefully or he was just a fast learner. All that natural athleticism of his was unleashed, and when the music began and he took her by the hand, everything clicked.

She twirled and swooped and he met her. He became her shadow, her other half, her mirror image. They touched, then broke away and returned to meet each other again.

The music swelled and, at one point, Darcy realized that people were watching them, but she didn't care. Patrick was totally focused on her, and she couldn't take her eyes off him.

When the music rose to a crescendo, he took her hand, twirling her around three times, then pulling her toward him in one fast, fluid movement. She rolled into him, pressing her palm and forearm flat against his chest in a controlled, sensual movement as she slid closer into his body, then pushed off of him, rolling backward and motioning to him in a come-hither gesture. He followed her, sliding on one knee to meet her and drawing her to him for a slow, swirling embrace as the music faded away.

The applause was instantaneous, and Darcy blinked. Her heart was pounding, and she looked at Patrick, not at the gathered guests.

He had stood and he was staring down at her, his hair falling over one brow, his green gaze intent.

"Let's get out of here," he whispered and she nodded.

"That was wonderful," someone called.

"Beautiful," someone else added.

"The sexiest thing I've ever seen between two people who are fully clothed," another person said.

"Oh, come on, take a bow," someone finally said.

Patrick looked askance at Darcy. "Your audience," he said.

"And yours." She tipped her head to him. "All right."

"Thank you," she called to the crowd as Patrick twirled her around one last time and nodded to his friends.

"Hey, you're not stealing her away, are you, Patrick?"

"Sorry, Cinderella and I need to rest," he called.

Out of the corner of her eye Darcy saw Angelise watching them, but she didn't come close. Then, Patrick opened the door, and the two of them moved out into the darkness beneath the stars. "That was amazing," Darcy said.

"*You* were amazing. You astound me. Constantly."

They wandered farther into the empty gardens, down a lonely trail lit only by small solar lanterns. The roses were dark shadows in the night.

"I astound you because…I'm not hiding from the world anymore?" Okay, she was pushing him, but that was the thing she wanted him to key in on, that she wasn't hiding. He didn't have to be concerned about that aspect of her life from now on.

His chuckle was incredibly sexy in the darkness. She couldn't see him clearly and the sound slipped through her bones, touching her and turning her to fire.

"When you decide to do something, you don't do it in a small way, do you?" he asked.

She smiled, but then realizing that he probably couldn't see her, either, pulled up short. He dropped to a bench on the path and she drew up beside him. "It wasn't so much that I decided," she whispered. "It was that you made it easy for me. You never treated me like an oddity."

"Why should I? You're a beautiful, intelligent and talented woman. That's not odd. It's pretty darn great."

"Thank you, but…even before you knew much about me, you saw me in a different light than other people had."

"You underestimate your ability to impress," he said. "I always knew that you were special."

Darcy closed her eyes. She wanted nothing more than to tell him that he was special, too, that she had loved him for longer than she had even realized, but that was the opposite of what she needed to do. She had come a long way to make a point and she wasn't trying hard enough, so she took his big hand in both of her own. She faced him in the darkness.

"You've given me so much, Patrick and I'm so…so incredibly grateful, but I want you to know that I'm much more confident now than I was when we met. I owe you for that, but you don't have to champion me or protect me anymore. I can do that on my own." Even as she was saying the words, she knew that this was her farewell to him, the last time she would see him. Angelise—or someone like her—was waiting in the wings, and that was as it should be, but that didn't make the pain in Darcy's heart any less powerful.

"I don't want you to be grateful."

"But I am." She could barely get the words past the ache in her throat. "Thanks to you I'm ready to proceed on my own. I don't have to have you beside me anymore."

"Dammit, Darcy." He leaned forward and framed her face. He brought his lips to hers.

The fire was instantaneous. She twisted closer, looping her arms around his neck.

"I've missed you," he said, and he kissed her again. Darcy's consciousness began to retreat. In a minute she was going to beg him to make love to her. She should stop now.

Instead she pressed into him. I missed you, too, she thought, but somehow she managed not to say the words. If she said them, if she even let him discern one tiny inkling of how she felt about him, he was going to feel so guilty eventually. Because he had that damned innate sense of duty.

Closing her eyes, Darcy breathed him in. She pushed back.

"I—I have to go. This is—" Heavenly, wonderful, everything I want. "It's wonderful," she said, deciding for honesty, "but not the right thing for me."

He stared at her, his chest heaving. "Of course," he finally said. "I'll see you to your room."

All right, she had to say it, to do it. She had to make the break.

"By leaving, I didn't actually mean my room. I'm going home. It's a bit early, but—" And there she stopped. Her throat began to clog with tears and she couldn't proceed. She had meant to tell him that she would be leaving Able House, too, but—she couldn't tell him. Nor could she stay at Able House waiting for him, knowing that she was going to turn into one of those many women who followed Patrick with their eyes, hoping for a few kisses and wishing for things that could never be.

She should at least tell him of her intent to find a new home in another part of the country. She owed him that much, but the words would have to wait for an e-mail or a letter. As it was, she was barely able to retain her faux composure.

"Say something," she said. "Tell me goodbye. Wish me a— a great flight home."

"You're leaving because I kissed you again. I took things for granted and pushed you," he said.

"No. I wanted you to kiss me."

"And now you want to leave."

No. She didn't want to leave at all. "I just need to leave." And it was all she could do not to beg him for one last kiss.

He stood, and she realized that this was the last walk they

would take together. Her heart hurt, her throat ached, her eyes…she would never make it back to the hotel without crying.

Dammit, yes, she would. She wasn't coming this far only to mess everything up at the end. So, they moved in silence to the door, he rode up to her room with her in the elevator. "When is your flight?" he asked.

"Tonight," she said. "I have a limo booked to take me to the airport." Both lies. Her plane left in the morning, so there was no limo tonight. But there would be. If she had to, she would sleep at the airport, because she didn't trust herself to stay in the same hotel as Patrick and not do something that would spoil all the progress she'd made.

Now, she had only one more thing she had to do before she severed her ties with Patrick forever and looked for a job in another town.

"I have a favor to ask of you," she said, forcing the words out. "I have an—an event planned for next Saturday. It's a bit different in scope from my usual, and you've always given me good feedback. I'd like to ask for your opinion on this, too."

He cleared his throat. "Ask." His voice was like a bullet, fast and hard and devoid of emotion.

"We'll have a live feed. If you're willing, I can set up a transmission. I'll send you a message with the details."

"That must be some event if you're transmitting it."

She nodded. "It's the biggest thing I've done yet."

He nodded. "I see. Yes, of course. You're moving up and on and this will be your big break. I promise you I'll watch, and I'll contact you afterward."

No. Don't contact me, she wanted to say. Don't tell me you'll call. If you do, I'll wait for the phone to ring. I'll die every time it rings and it isn't you, and if you call and I hear the sound of your voice…

The unthinkable might happen. If she didn't make the break clean, she'd be begging him to come back and let her work in his kitchen again, and she would suffer far too much when he finally settled down and started looking for a bride.

It was time to go. This was it. The last time she would ever see him.

"Patrick."

He knelt by her side.

"Are you making yourself small for me again?" she whispered.

"No, I'm bringing myself close."

"I'm glad." She threw caution to the wind and risked eternal heartbreak as she reached for him and kissed him with all her heart. Then, without saying goodbye, she let herself in her room.

One hour later, she left the hotel. Her heart stayed behind.

CHAPTER FIFTEEN

PATRICK had been in a bad mood for days, and he wasn't sure why. Or…maybe he *was* sure why, and that was the problem. He'd just discovered something about himself. He was in love with a woman he couldn't have.

That brief visit of Darcy's should have reassured him and helped get her out of his system. She was well, she was beyond well. She was vivacious and outgoing and sparkling and…she had absolutely no need of him anymore. Her life had moved beyond him. He should be happy for her.

He was. He also missed her like crazy.

And as the day for her televised event came close, he turned into a ragged fool, forgetting to sleep or eat. He forgot duty. He missed an appointment for the first time in his career.

Now, he sat in the dark, private auditorium and waited tensely for Darcy to appear on the screen.

And then she was there. But…what was she doing?

Patrick sat up straighter. He leaned forward in his chair.

Darcy moved to the center of a makeshift stage. She held a microphone, and while she was getting ready to speak, the camera panned over the crowd in front of the stage. The area dead in the center was crowded with people in wheelchairs, far more than the Able House residents could account for. But beyond that, Patrick made out his sisters, what looked to be most if not all of his neighbors, friends and even some politicians. Camera crews from local television stations were in evidence.

The camera zoomed in on Darcy again. Dressed in pale yellow with that smile, that incredible smile he loved, she was riveting. Patrick couldn't have looked away if the roof of the auditorium had caved in. A banner behind her came into view. It read, The First Annual Patrick Judson Able House Festival.

Patrick swore beneath his breath.

Darcy cleared her throat. "First of all, let me welcome all of you and thank you for coming. Today is a day that heralds what will, hopefully, become a new tradition in the city and in this neighborhood. In a few moments, we'll begin a day of competitions, classes, food, fun and togetherness, and all of that has been made possible by Patrick Judson who spearheaded Able House and served as an intermediary between us and the community.

"Unfortunately Patrick can't be with us today. He's in France but he's watching us and I know that he's here in spirit. It was Patrick's idea to have those of us at Able House share our skills with the community, and as a result, we're now involved in a community education program teaching evening classes as well as participating in an enrichment program at the local grammar schools twice a month. Patrick's idea has proven to be so successful and popular that we've decided to take it to the next step. We don't just want to live in this community, we want to be a vital part of it, so to that end, for the past two weeks we've fanned out into the community to approach our neighbors and invite those who were willing to come here today to share their talents with all of us. The result is this community festival. In addition, we'll be opening our doors one weekend and one weeknight a month so that we can all join together for classes, book discussions and a meal.

"All of this has been made possible by those on both sides who have been willing to reach out to each other. When we first came here, many people were skeptical and nervous, but you've welcomed us and now we welcome *you* into our home. We're so glad to have you here."

The crowd broke into applause. Someone called out, "Way to go, Darcy!"

She waved and held out her hand for silence. "And now, I have just one last thing I want to add before we begin and that is this: "Patrick, wherever you are, we're—we miss you."

Patrick had moved from his chair and was standing directly in front of the huge screen now, staring into a larger than life Darcy's eyes. Those beautiful eyes were filled with unshed tears and her voice had broken.

She had never been more beautiful. His heart had never hurt this hard.

"We miss you," she continued, "and all of us here at Able House want to thank you for…for enriching our lives, for championing us, but mostly for helping us and the world to realize that each of us, every one of us in the world, whether on two legs or four wheels, have gifts to give, and those gifts are meant to be shared with others. I'll—*I'll* miss you," she finished. Her last words were barely a whisper.

Were those tears streaming down her face? Undoubtedly.

Patrick moved closer, but—dammit—this was just a screen. The real Darcy was a continent away. He heard her whisper, "I—I need to make the sendoff announcement, but—I—would you please do it for me?"

A gruff male voice said something Patrick couldn't understand. Then Cal Barrow appeared on stage and took the microphone from Darcy. She moved out of view.

Outrage filled Patrick's soul. What was that guy doing forcing Darcy off the stage?

Patrick whipped out his cell phone. He started to call his sister and had hit the first three numbers when Cal cleared his throat.

"It's time to get started, folks," he said. "The schedules are on the table, the food is in the dining room, events are in the rooms, in the lobby, on the stage, in the pool and out on the lawns. Go to it and have a great time. Oh, and—could we please give a cheer for Darcy and Mr. Judson? She's made me crazy and I've been a total ass. Me and Billings—who has, thank goodness, decided to move—were the lone holdouts and were pretty mean to Darcy and everyone here, but…what can I say? She knows how to win a guy over and make him feel like a stupid heel and now she's got me teaching woodcarving, so…let the games begin!"

The crowd exploded in applause.

People were starting to file out to wherever they were going, cutting in front of the cameras and such when Cal fiddled with the mike again. "Oh, and Judson? If you're wondering how a little bit of a woman who took me down and punched me in the unmentionables managed to make a believer out of me…she got me with her brownies. Came over every damn day for nine days and brought a different kind every day. I cursed her up and down and all she would say was, 'Cal, don't make me hit you again. Do you want a brownie or not?' So, the fact is…I don't know how you can stay away from her. She's a hard one to ignore. She's a total bully and a sweetheart, too. Makes me want to beat *myself* up for what I did to her and all the fine people here."

Then the mike went dead.

The screen broke into four areas, each one covering a different event taking place on the grounds. Every thirty seconds the areas would switch in a round robin random kaleidoscope. There was a group of knitters, a film discussion group, Cal's woodcarving, relay races with teams alternating a racer on foot with a racer in a wheelchair, a photography group, swimmers, a homemade miniature golf course and numerous other activities. Patrick was impressed, but despite the ever-changing footage and the fact that he had seen almost everyone else, his sisters waving to the camera as they assisted at the races and in the pool, the woman he wanted most to see eluded him.

Patrick cursed the cameramen who didn't seem to know what was important. Once again he took out his phone. Surely one of his sisters could remedy the situation. This time he got Lane.

"I miss you. I love you. Where the hell is she?" he asked.

"Whoa, Patrick," Lane said. "Who is *she?*"

"Darcy."

"Ah."

"Don't ah me, Lane. I need help."

"Sounds like you need Darcy."

"Yes."

"I might tell you if you stop being so cranky. Darcy and Cara and Amy and I have bonded while you've been gone."

"That's great." He meant it, too.

"She knows you almost as well as we do."

"You might be right about that, but…*where is she?*"

"How's Angelise?" Lane suddenly asked.

"I don't know. I don't care. Where's Darcy?"

Lane chuckled. "Right answer, big brother. She's been cooking and other stuff. I'll get a cameraman over to her."

"Thank you, Lane. I do love you."

"Me, too. Just…be careful. I don't want to see you get hurt."

"What do you mean?"

"Darcy's leaving soon. She's moving to Seattle. She told me last night."

Patrick's heart fell right onto the floor and shattered at his feet. He clicked off the phone. He ignored the ringing when it began. He watched as the camera zoomed in on Darcy. She was sitting on a couch reading a story…and she had a toddler on her lap. Davey and Charlie were snuggled up beside her. She was surrounded by children. As she read the story, something about a bunny, she smiled at something Davey said and leaned over and dropped a kiss on his head.

Patrick felt as if he was going to collapse. His Darcy had mastered her demons. She was happy.

She was leaving. And she hadn't told him.

For a long time he sat there. The screen flickered as the cameras switched from room to room, except the one on Darcy never moved.

His phone rang again. He answered it.

"Patrick?" Lane's voice was worried.

"I'm all right," he said. But he wasn't.

"You didn't know that she was leaving, did you?" she asked.

"I know now."

"Do you care?"

"Lane, let's talk later. I have something to do now." He was already starting to move by the time he clicked the phone off. Within hours he was flying over the Atlantic.

Darcy awoke with a headache and a deep sense of sadness and distress. Yesterday had gone well, but she hadn't heard from Patrick. Lane had mentioned that she spoke with him briefly, but that was all.

So, there was nothing left to do but make her final arrangements to depart. Patrick's new life had obviously taken hold. She had to make her own way, too.

That's what she should get started on. Definitely. It would be the height of stupidity hanging around today hoping that he would call so that she could say goodbye to him.

"You call him," she told herself, but she knew that she wouldn't do that.

Listlessly she took a shower and got dressed. She opened her door and went out into the hallway.

Patrick was leaning against the wall opposite her room, his arms and ankles crossed. He didn't smile when he saw her.

Her heart leaped, then fell.

"What's wrong? Why are you here?" she finally asked.

"When were you going to tell me?" he asked, pushing off the wall.

"Tell you…"

"Lane said that you were moving to Seattle and…dammit, Darcy, not a word? Not a hint? Why?"

"I—I thought you might worry about why I was going." But, of course, that was only part of the truth.

"You're darned right I'm worried. Did we run you off? Did something happen? I know it wasn't Cal, because he seems to have fallen totally under your spell. What happened?"

You, she wanted to say. Just you. Love.

"I—well, I'm not so scared of being out and about in public anymore and I—"

"That's no reason." He ran his hand through his hair. "Or…maybe it's a perfectly good reason. I shouldn't be badgering you. It's your life. You're free to live it the way you want to."

No. No, she wasn't. Darcy bit her lip.

"You're supposed to be in France," she said.

"I was. Now I'm here."

"Why?"

"I had to see you. I was afraid you would leave and I wouldn't be able to find you. I had to tell you...thank you for yesterday. You were magnificent. You've accomplished so much. Seattle is going to love you."

He crossed the hall, reached out and gently touched her face. "Not half as much as I do, but they'll adore you."

Darcy froze. Yearning swept through her and she looked up, his fingertips sliding across her jaw. His touch was heaven. Love? Had he said love? Did he mean—?

No, of course not. He'd meant it in a generic way, like "I love cookies." Not "I love you so much that it kills me to be apart from you."

That kind of love and hurt was what she was feeling right now. The kind that made your throat hurt and your eyes sting. She was staring into those green eyes that did awful, wonderful things to her and she felt herself falling apart.

"Don't go," he said, in a ragged, broken voice.

She closed her eyes. "I have to. I can't stay here."

"Why?"

Again she looked into his eyes. "You have a plan for your life. You've had it for years. It's a good plan, a great plan, a totally wonderful plan. You have things to do overseas. There are people counting on you. You're the center of everything happening there. And you want it. You've always wanted it, and I want you to have it, too. More than anything." She bit her lip, fought the tears.

Patrick dropped to his knees in front of her. "That plan of mine? It *was* a good plan, Darcy, but plans change. You came into my life and changed everything."

"No!"

"Yes. I can hire people for France and Spain. I have money to pay people to take my place everywhere but here. With you."

"You wanted to be free. I want you to be free."

"I love you, Darcy. Being apart from you taught me that freedom is so much more than being alone. Being *with* you frees me. You opened my eyes to pathways I hadn't even imagined. All those years ago when my parents died and left me alone to raise my sisters, I thought I needed my freedom, but what I needed, what I wanted, was someone to share my life. Someone to talk to and love as an equal. What I wanted, Darcy, was you."

"Patrick…"

He placed two fingers over her lips. "You don't have to let me down easy. Just tell me if I have any chance of convincing you to stay, yes or no."

He opened his mouth to say something more, but she leaned forward and placed her fingers over *his* lips this time.

"I love you, Patrick," she said. "Just in case it isn't shining through in my eyes." She leaned forward and wrapped her arms around his neck.

"Is that a yes, you'll stay, Darcy?"

"It's the loudest yes you'll ever hear. I've missed you so much. You complete me. You make me want to do more and be more than I've ever been."

Patrick drew her close and kissed her. "You don't have to be more," he said. "You're already everything I want and need."

EPILOGUE

Six months later, Patrick came in to find Darcy baby-sitting Charlie and Davey. She gave them each a hug, then sent them over to Patrick for more hugs before they ran off to find Olivia in the kitchen.

"They're so precious," she said. "Your sisters have let me hog them lately. I wonder what Amy and Cara and Lane will think when they find out there's a new Judson on the way." Darcy looked down at her still flat abdomen.

Patrick kissed her. "I suppose they'll be just as happy to hear about the baby as they were when they found out you were marrying me. And then they'll probably take turns filling in the calendar so they can baby-sit."

Darcy looked up at him, a slight trace of concern in those lovely eyes. "I hope I'll be a good mother," she said.

Patrick did a double take and raised one eyebrow. "Have you ever found anything you're not good at? Since we got married, you've mastered downhill skiing and wheelchair tennis and probably a few other things I've forgotten about. If I hadn't begged you to consider my heart and not take up skydiving you probably would have excelled at that, too. Do you seriously believe you won't be a good mother?"

She reached out and slid one hand around his neck, pulling him close for a quick kiss. "I'm so glad I met you."

Patrick smiled. "Me, too. From the minute I walked into the kitchen and found you defying me, I was lost."

"I was, too, even though I didn't think I'd survive you. I didn't think I'd ever want to have a child, either, but...do you think we might have more than one?"

What did I ever do to deserve this woman? Patrick thought. "Yes," he said. "Absolutely."

He laughed.

"What?" she asked.

"You," he said. "You have so much energy, so much love, so much life. I can't imagine why I ever thought I needed to go looking for adventure when living with you is the greatest adventure of my life."

"What a catch you are," she said with a teasing smile.

"Does that mean I get to kiss you again?"

"It means a whole lot of things. I'll show you later," she said. "After everyone has gone home. It's going to take a little while."

"Hours?" he asked, raising one eyebrow.

"Years," she said with a mocking smile and love in her eyes. "At least fifty. Now, kiss me, please."

He did. Then he smiled against her lips.

"What?" she asked.

"Kissing you has to be a whole lot better than flying," he confessed.

She kissed him again. "Let the adventure begin, love," she said.

Oh, but it already had. And it was so much better than he'd ever dreamed.

MILLS & BOON

Pure reading pleasure™

JUNE 2009 HARDBACK TITLES

ROMANCE

The Sicilian's Baby Bargain	Penny Jordan
Mistress: Pregnant by the Spanish Billionaire	Kim Lawrence
Bound by the Marcolini Diamonds	Melanie Milburne
Blackmailed into the Greek Tycoon's Bed	Carol Marinelli
The Ruthless Greek's Virgin Princess	Trish Morey
Veretti's Dark Vengeance	Lucy Gordon
Spanish Magnate, Red-Hot Revenge	Lynn Raye Harris
Argentinian Playboy, Unexpected Love-Child	Chantelle Shaw
The Savakis Mistress	Annie West
Captive in the Millionaire's Castle	Lee Wilkinson
Cattle Baron: Nanny Needed	Margaret Way
Greek Boss, Dream Proposal	Barbara McMahon
Boardroom Baby Surprise	Jackie Braun
Bachelor Dad on Her Doorstep	Michelle Douglas
Hired: Cinderella Chef	Myrna Mackenzie
Miss Maple and the Playboy	Cara Colter
A Special Kind of Family	Marion Lennox
Hot Shot Surgeon, Cinderella Bride	Alison Roberts

HISTORICAL

The Rake's Wicked Proposal	Carole Mortimer
The Transformation of Miss Ashworth	Anne Ashley
Mistress Below Deck	Helen Dickson

MEDICAL™

Emergency: Wife Lost and Found	Carol Marinelli
A Summer Wedding at Willowmere	Abigail Gordon
The Playboy Doctor Claims His Bride	Janice Lynn
Miracle: Twin Babies	Fiona Lowe

MILLS & BOON®

Pure reading pleasure™

JUNE 2009 LARGE PRINT TITLES

ROMANCE

The Ruthless Magnate's Virgin Mistress	Lynne Graham
The Greek's Forced Bride	Michelle Reid
The Sheikh's Rebellious Mistress	Sandra Marton
The Prince's Waitress Wife	Sarah Morgan
The Australian's Society Bride	Margaret Way
The Royal Marriage Arrangement	Rebecca Winters
Two Little Miracles	Caroline Anderson
Manhattan Boss, Diamond Proposal	Trish Wylie

HISTORICAL

Marrying the Mistress	Juliet Landon
To Deceive a Duke	Amanda McCabe
Knight of Grace	Sophia James

MEDICAL™

A Mummy for Christmas	Caroline Anderson
A Bride and Child Worth Waiting For	Marion Lennox
One Magical Christmas	Carol Marinelli
The GP's Meant-To-Be Bride	Jennifer Taylor
The Italian Surgeon's Christmas Miracle	Alison Roberts
Children's Doctor, Christmas Bride	Lucy Clark

0609 Gen Std HB

ROMANCE

Marchese's Forgotten Bride	Michelle Reid
The Brazilian Millionaire's Love-Child	Anne Mather
Powerful Greek, Unworldly Wife	Sarah Morgan
The Virgin Secretary's Impossible Boss	Carole Mortimer
Kyriakis's Innocent Mistress	Diana Hamilton
Rich, Ruthless and Secretly Royal	Robyn Donald
Spanish Aristocrat, Forced Bride	India Grey
Kept for Her Baby	Kate Walker
The Costanzo Baby Secret	Catherine Spencer
The Mediterranean's Wife by Contract	Kathryn Ross
Claimed: Secret Royal Son	Marion Lennox
Expecting Miracle Twins	Barbara Hannay
A Trip with the Tycoon	Nicola Marsh
Invitation to the Boss's Ball	Fiona Harper
Keeping Her Baby's Secret	Raye Morgan
Memo: The Billionaire's Proposal	Melissa McClone
Secret Sheikh, Secret Baby	Carol Marinelli
The Playboy Doctor's Surprise Proposal	Anne Fraser

HISTORICAL

The Piratical Miss Ravenhurst	Louise Allen
His Forbidden Liaison	Joanna Maitland
An Innocent Debutante in Hanover Square	Anne Herries

MEDICAL™

Pregnant Midwife: Father Needed	Fiona McArthur
His Baby Bombshell	Jessica Matthews
Found: A Mother for His Son	Dianne Drake
Hired: GP and Wife	Judy Campbell

0609 Gen Std LP

™ MILLS & BOON®

Pure reading pleasure™

JULY 2009 LARGE PRINT TITLES

ROMANCE

Captive At The Sicilian Billionaire's Command	Penny Jordan
The Greek's Million-Dollar Baby Bargain	Julia James
Bedded for the Spaniard's Pleasure	Carole Mortimer
At the Argentinean Billionaire's Bidding	India Grey
Italian Groom, Princess Bride	Rebecca Winters
Falling for her Convenient Husband	Jessica Steele
Cinderella's Wedding Wish	Jessica Hart
The Rebel Heir's Bride	Patricia Thayer

HISTORICAL

The Rake's Defiant Mistress	Mary Brendan
The Viscount Claims His Bride	Bronwyn Scott
The Major and the Country Miss	Dorothy Elbury

MEDICAL™

The Greek Doctor's New-Year Baby	Kate Hardy
The Heart Surgeon's Secret Child	Meredith Webber
The Midwife's Little Miracle	Fiona McArthur
The Single Dad's New-Year Bride	Amy Andrews
The Wife He's Been Waiting For	Dianne Drake
Posh Doc Claims His Bride	Anne Fraser